Hans Brinker, or The Silver Skates

Hans Brinker, or The Silver Skates

MARY MAPES DODGE

WITH ILLUSTRATIONS BY ALICE CARSEY

COSIMO CLASSICS

NEW YORK

Hans Brinker, or The Silver Skates
© 2005 Cosimo, Inc.

Cosimo, P.O. Box 416
Old Chelsea Station
New York, NY 10113-0416

or visit our website at:
www.cosimobooks.com

Hans Brinker, or The Silver Skates originally published by
Whitman Publishing Co. in 1865.

Library of Congress Cataloging-in-Publication Data
A catalog record for this book is available from the Library of Congress

Cover design by www.wiselephant.com

ISBN: 1-59605-415-8

THEIR MOTHER'S TALL FORM STOOD IN THE DOORWAY

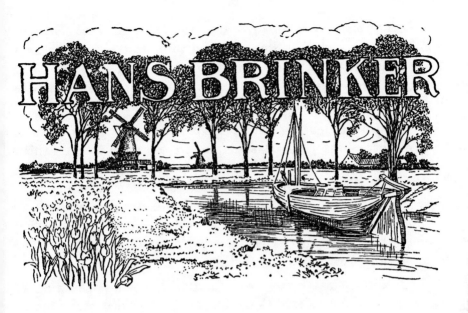

I

HANS AND GRETEL

ON a bright December morning, long ago, two thinly clad children were kneeling upon the bank of a frozen canal in Holland.

The sun had not yet appeared, but the gray sky was parted near the horizon and its edges shone crimson with the coming day. Most of the good Hollanders were enjoying a placid morning nap; even Mynheer von Stoppelnoze, that worthy old Dutchman, was still slumbering "in beautiful repose."

Now and then some peasant woman, poising a well filled basket upon her head, came skimming over the glassy surface of the canal; or a lusty boy, skating to his day's work in the town, cast a good-natured grimace toward the shivering pair as he flew along.

Meanwhile, with many a vigorous pull, the brother and sister, for such they were, seemed to be fastening something upon their feet—not skates, certainly, but clumsy pieces of wood narrowed and smoothed at their lower edge, and pierced with holes through which were threaded strings of raw-hide.

These queer looking affairs had been made by the boy Hans. His mother was a poor peasant-woman, too poor to even think of such a thing as buying skates for her little ones. Rough as these were, they had afforded the children many a happy hour upon the ice; and now as with cold, red fingers our young Hollanders tugged at the strings—their solemn faces bending closely over their knees—no vision of impossible iron runners came to dull the satisfaction within.

In a moment the boy arose, and with a pompous swing of the arms, and a careless "Come on, Gretel!" glided easily across the canal.

"Ah, Hans," called his sister plaintively, "this foot is not well yet. The strings hurt me on last Market day; and now I cannot bear them tied in the same place."

"Tie them higher up, then," answered Hans, as without looking at her he performed a wonderful cat's-cradle step on the ice.

"How can I? The string is too short."

Giving vent to a good-natured Dutch whistle, the English of which was that girls were troublesome creatures, he steered toward her.

"You are foolish to wear such shoes, Gretel, when you have a stout leather pair. Your wooden shoes would be better than these."

"Why, Hans! Do you forget? The father threw my beautiful new shoes into the fire. Before I knew what he had done they were all curled up in the midst of the burning peat. I can skate with these, but not with my wooden ones.—Be careful now—"

Hans had taken a string from his pocket. Humming a tune as he knelt beside her, he proceeded to fasten Gretel's skate with all the force of his strong young arm.

"Oh! oh!" she cried, in real pain

With an impatient jerk Hans unwound the string. He would have cast it upon the ground in true big-brother style, had he not just then spied a tear trickling down his sister's cheek.

"I'll fix it—never fear," he said, with sudden tenderness, "but we must be quick; the mother will need us soon."

Then he glanced inquiringly about him, first at the ground, next at some bare willow branches above his head, and finally at the sky now gorgeous with streaks of blue, crimson and gold.

Finding nothing in any of these localities to meet his need, his eye suddenly brightened as, with the air of a fellow who knew what he was about, he took off his cap and, removing the tattered lining, adjusted it in a smooth pad over the top of Gretel's worn-out shoe.

"Now," he cried, triumphantly, at the same time arranging the strings as briskly as his benumbed fingers would allow, "can you bear some pulling?"

Gretel drew up her lips as if to say, "Hurt away," but made no further response.

In another moment they were laughing together, as hand in hand they flew along the canal, never thinking whether the ice would bear or not, for in Holland ice is generally an all-winter affair.

Presently, squeak! squeak! sounded something beneath Hans' feet. Next his strokes grew shorter, ending oft-times with a jerk, and finally he lay sprawling upon the ice, kicking against the air with many a fantastic flourish.

"Ha! ha!" laughed Gretel, "that was a fine tumble!" But a tender heart was beating under her coarse blue jacket and, even as she laughed, she came, with a graceful sweep, close to her prostrate brother.

"Are you hurt, Hans? Oh, you are laughing! Catch me now!"—and she darted away, shivering no longer, but with cheeks all aglow and eyes sparkling with fun.

Hans sprang to his feet and started in brisk pursuit, but it was no easy thing to catch Gretel. Before she had traveled very far, her skates, too, began to squeak.

Believing that discretion was the better part of valor, she turned suddenly and skated into her pursuer's arms.

"Ha! ha! I've caught you!" cried Han

"Ha! ha! I caught *you!*" she retorted, struggling to free herself.

Just then a clear, quick voice was heard calling, "Hans! Gretel!"

"It's the mother," said Hans, looking solemn in an instant.

By this time the canal was gilded with sunlight. The pure morning air was very delightful and skaters were gradually increasing in numbers. It was hard to obey the summons. But Hans and Gretel were good children; without a thought of yielding to the temptation to linger, they pulled off their skates, leaving half the knots still tied. Hans, with his great square shoulders and bushy yellow hair, towered high above his blue-eyed little sister, as they trudged homeward. He was fifteen years old and Gretel was only twelve. He was a solid, hearty-looking boy, with honest eyes. Gretel was lithe and quick; her eyes had a dancing light in them, and while you looked at her cheek the color paled and deepened just as it does upon a bed of pink and white blossoms when the wind is blowing.

As soon as the children turned from the canal they could see their parents' cottage. Their mother's tall form, arrayed in jacket and petticoat and close-fitting cap, stood, like a picture, in the crooked frame of the doorway. Had the cottage been a mile away, it would still have seemed near. In that flat country every object stands out plainly in the distance; the chickens show as distinctly as the windmills. Indeed, were it not for the dykes and the high banks of the canals, one could stand almost anywhere in middle Holland without seeing a mound or a ridge between the eye and the "jumping-off place."

None had better cause to know the nature of these same dykes than Dame Brinker, because her husband had worked on them for years. It was at the time of a threatened inundation, when in the midst of a terrible storm, in darkness and sleet, the men were laboring at a weak spot near the Veermyk sluice, that he fell from the scaffolding and was taken home insensible. From that hour he never worked again; though he lived on, mind and memory were gone.

Gretel could not remember him otherwise than as the strange, silent man, whose eyes followed her vacantly whichever way she turned; but Hans had recollections of a hearty, cheer-ful-voiced father who was never tired of bearing him upon his shoulder, and whose careless song still seemed echoing near when he lay awake at night and listened.

"DON'T YOU HEAR THE LAST BELL? CATCH ME!"

II

DAME BRINKER earned a scanty support for her family by raising vegetables, spinning and knitting. Once she had worked on board the barges plying up and down the canal, and had occasionally been harnessed with other women to the towing rope of a water dray plying between Broek and Amsterdam. But when Hans had grown strong and large, he had insisted upon doing all such drudgery in her place. Besides, her husband had become so very helpless of late that he required her constant care. Although not having as much intelligence as a little child, he was yet strong of arm and very hearty, and Dame Brinker had sometimes great trouble in controlling him.

"Ah! children, he was so good and steady," she would sometimes say, "and as wise as a lawyer. Even the Burgomaster would stop to ask him a question, and now, alack! he don't know his wife and little ones. You remember the father, Hans, when he was himself—a great, brave man—don't you?"

"Yes, indeed, mother; he knew everything and could do anything under the sun—and how he would sing! Why, you used to laugh and say it was enough to set the windmills dancing."

"So I did. Bless me! how the boy remembers! Gretel, child, take that knitting needle from your father, quick; he'll get it in his eyes maybe; and put the shoe on him. His poor

15

feet are like ice half the time, but I can't keep 'em covered all I can do—" and then, half wailing, half humming, Dame Brinker would sit down and fill the low cottage with the whirr of her spinning wheel.

Nearly all the outdoor work, as well as the household labor, was performed by Hans and Gretel. At certain seasons of the year the children went out day after day to gather peat, which they would stow away in square, brick-like pieces, for fuel. At other times, when home-work permitted, Hans rode the towing-horses on the canals, earning a few cents a day; and Gretel tended the geese for the neighboring farmers.

Hans was clever at carving in wood, and both he and Gretel were good gardeners. Gretel could sing and sew and run on great, high, home-made stilts better than any girl for miles around. She could learn a ballad in five minutes, and find, in its season, any weed or flower you could name; but she dreaded books, and often the very sight of the figuring-board in the old school-house would set her eyes swimming. Hans, on the contrary, was slow and steady. The harder the task, whether in study or daily labor, the better he liked it. Boys who sneered at him out of school, on account of his patched clothes and scant leather breeches, were forced to yield him the post of honor in nearly every class. It was not long before he was the only youngster in the school who had not stood at least *once* in the corner of horrors, where hung a dreaded whip, and over it this motto: "Learn, learn! you idler, or this rope's end shall teach you."

It was only in winter that Gretel and Hans could be spared to attend school; and for the past month they had been kept at home because their mother needed their services. Raff Brinker required constant attention and there was black bread to be made, and the house to be kept clean, and stockings and other things to be knitted and sold in the market place.

While they were busily assisting their mother on this cold December morning, a merry troop of girls and boys came skimming down the canal. There were fine skaters among them, and as the bright medley of costumes flitted by it looked from a distance as though the ice had suddenly thawed and some gay tulip-bed were floating along on the current.

There was the rich Burgomaster's daughter, Hilda van Gleck, with her costly furs and loose-fitting velvet sacque; and, near by, a pretty peasant girl, Annie Bouman, jauntily attired in a coarse scarlet jacket and a blue skirt just short enough to display the gray homespun hose to advantage. Then there was the proud Rychie van Korbes, whose father, Mynheer van Korbes, was one of the leading men of Amsterdam; and, flocking closely around her, Carl Schummel, Peter and Ludwig van Holp, Jacob Poot, and a very small boy rejoicing in the tremendous name of Voostenwalbert Schimmelpenninck. There were nearly twenty other boys and girls in the party, and one and all seemed full of excitement and frolic.

Suddenly the whole party came to a standstill and, grouping themselves out of the way of the passers-by, all talked at once to a pretty little maiden, whom they had drawn from the tide of people flowing toward the town.

"Oh, Katrinka!" they cried, in a breath, "have you heard of it? The race—we want you to join!"

"What race?" asked Katrinka, laughing. "Don't all talk at once, please; I can't understand."

Every one panted and looked at Rychie van Korbes, who was their acknowledged spokeswoman.

"Why," said Rychie, "we are to have a grand skating match

on the twentieth, on Mevrouw van Gleck's birthday. It's all
Hilda's work. They are going to give a splendid prize to the
best skater."

"Yes," chimed in a half-a-dozen voices, "a beautiful pair
of silver skates—perfectly magnificent! with, oh! such straps and
silver bells and buckles!"

"*Who* said they had bells?" put in the small voice of the
boy with the big name.

"*I* say so, Master Voost," replied Rychie.

. "So they have—" "No, I'm sure they haven't—" "*Oh,*
how can you say so?—" "It's an arrow—" "and Mynheer van
Korbes told *my* mother they had bells—" came from sundry of
the excited group; but Mynheer Voostenwalbert Schimmelpenninck essayed to settle the matter with a decisive—

"Well, you don't any of you know a single thing about it;
they haven't a sign of a bell on them; they—"

"Oh! oh!" and the chorus of conflicting opinion broke forth
again.

"The girls' pair are to have bells," interposed Hilda, quietly,
"but there is to be another pair for the boys with an arrow
engraved upon the sides."

"*There!* I told you so!" cried nearly all the youngsters in
a breath.

Katrinka looked at them with bewildered eyes.

"Who is to try?" she asked.

"All of us," answered Rychie. "It will be such fun! And
you must, too, Katrinka. But it's school time now; we will talk
it all over at noon. Oh! you will join, of course."

Katrinka, without replying, made a graceful pirouette, and,
laughing out a coquettish—"Don't you hear the last bell? Catch

me!"—darted off toward the school-house, standing half a mile away, on the canal.

All started, pell-mell, at this challenge, but they tried in vain to catch the bright-eyed, laughing creature who, with golden hair streaming in the sunlight, cast back many a sparkling glance of triumph as she floated onward.

Beautiful Katrinka! Flushed with youth and health, all life and mirth and motion, what wonder thine image, ever floating in advance, sped through one boy's dreams that night! What wonder that it seemed his darkest hour when, years afterward, thy presence floated away from him forever.

III

HANS AND GRETEL FIND A FRIEND

A T noon our young friends poured forth from the school-house
intent upon having an hour's practicing upon the canal

They had skated but a few moments when Carl Schummel
said mockingly to Hilda:

"There's a pretty pair just coming upon the ice! The little
rag-pickers! Their skates must have been a present from the
king direct."

"They are patient creatures," said Hilda, gently. "It must
have been hard to learn to skate upon such queer affairs. They
are very poor peasants, you see. The boy has probably made
the skates himself."

Carl was somewhat abashed.

"Patient they may be, but as for skating, they start off
pretty well only to finish with a jerk. They could move well
to your new *staccato* piece, I think."

Hilda laughed pleasantly and left him. After joining a
small detachment of the racers, and sailing past every one of
them, she halted beside Gretel, who, with eager eyes, had been
watching the sport.

"What is your name, little girl?"

"Gretel, my lady," answered the child, somewhat awed by
Hilda's rank, though they were nearly of the same age, "and
my brother is called Hans."

"Hans is a stout fellow," said Hilda, cheerily, "and seems to have a warm stove somewhere within him, but *you* look cold. You should wear more clothing, little one."

Gretel, who had nothing else to wear, tried to laugh as she answered:

"I am not so very little. I am past twelve years old."

"Oh, I beg your pardon. You see, I am nearly fourteen, and so large for my age that other girls seem small to me, but that is nothing. Perhaps you will shoot up far above me yet; not unless you dress more warmly, though—shivering girls never grow."

Hans flushed as he saw tears rising in Gretel's eyes.

"My sister has not complained of the cold; but this is bitter weather, they say—" and he looked sadly upon Gretel.

"It is nothing," said Gretel. "I am often warm—too warm when I am skating. You are good to think of it."

"No, no," answered Hilda, quite angry at herself. "I am careless, cruel, but I meant no harm. I wanted to ask you—I mean—if—" and here Hilda, coming to the point of her errand, faltered before the poorly clad but noble-looking children she wished to serve.

"What is it, young lady?" exclaimed Hans eagerly. "If there is any service I can do? any—"

"Oh! no, no," laughed Hilda, shaking off her embarrassment, "I only wished to speak to you about the grand race. Why do you not join it? You both can skate well, and the ranks are free. Any one may enter for the prize."

Gretel looked wistfully at Hans, who, tugging at his cap, answered respectfully:

"Ah, jufvrouw, even if we could enter, we could skate only

a few strokes with the rest. Our skates are hardwood, you see" (holding up the sole of his foot), "but they soon become damp and then they stick and trip us."

Gretel's eyes twinkled with fun as she thought of Hans' mishap in the morning, but she blushed as she faltered out timidly:

"Oh, no, we can't join; but may we be there, my lady, on the great day, to look on?"

"Certainly," answered Hilda, looking kindly into the two earnest faces and wishing from her heart that she had not spent so much of her monthly allowance for lace and finery. She had but eighty cents left, and that would buy but one pair of skates, at the furthest.

Looking down with a sigh at the two pair of feet so very different in size, she asked:

"Which of you is the better skater?"

"Gretel," replied Hans, promptly.

"Hans," answered Gretel, in the same breath.

Hilda smiled.

"I cannot buy you each a pair of skates, or even one good pair; but here is eighty cents. Decide between you which stands the best chance of winning the race, and buy the skates accordingly. I wish I had enough to buy better ones—goodbye!" and, with a nod and a smile, Hilda, after handing the money to the electrified Hans, glided swiftly away to rejoin her companions.

"Jufvrouw! Jufvrouw van Gleck!" called Hans in a loud tone, stumbling after her as well as he could, for one of his skate-strings was untied.

Hilda turned and, with one hand raised to shield her eyes

from the sun, seemed to him to be floating through the air, nearer and nearer.

"We cannot take this money," panted Hans, "though we know your goodness in giving it."

"Why not, indeed?" asked Hilda, flushing.

"Because," replied Hans, bowing like a clown, but looking with the eye of a prince at the queenly girl, "we have not earned it."

Hilda was quick-witted. She had noticed a pretty wooden chain upon Gretel's neck—

"Carve me a chain, Hans, like the one your sister wears."

"That I will, lady, with all my heart; we have white-wood in the house, fine as ivory; you shall have one tomorrow," and Hans hastily tried to return the money.

"No, no," said Hilda, decidedly. "That sum will be but a poor price for the chain," and off she darted, outstripping the fleetest among the skaters.

Hans sent a long, bewildered gaze after her; it was useless, he felt, to make any further resistance.

"It is right," he muttered, half to himself, half to his faithful shadow, Gretel; "I must work hard every minute, and sit up half the night, if the mother will let me burn a candle; but the chain shall be finished. We may keep the money, Gretel."

"What a good little lady!" cried Gretel, clapping her hands with delight; "Oh! Hans, was it for nothing the stork settled on our roof last summer? Do you remember how the mother said it would bring us luck, and how she cried when Janzoon Kolp shot him? And she said it would bring him trouble. But the luck has come to us at last! Now, Hans, if mother sends us to town tomorrow you can buy the skates in the market place."

Hans shook his head. "The young lady would have *given* us the money to buy skates, but if I *earn* it, Gretel, it shall be spent for wool. You must have a warm jacket."

"Oh!" cried Gretel, in real dismay, "not buy the skates! Why, I am not often cold! Mother says the blood runs up and down in poor children's veins, humming 'I must keep 'em warm! I must keep 'em warm.'

"Oh, Hans," she continued, with something like a sob, "don't say you won't buy the skates, it makes me feel just like crying—besides, I want to be cold—I mean I'm real, awful warm—so now!"

Hans looked up hurriedly. He had a true Dutch horror of tears, or emotion of any kind, and, most of all, he dreaded to see his sister's blue eyes overflowing.

"Now mind," cried Gretel, seeing her advantage, "I'll feel awful if you give up skates. *I* don't want them. I'm not such a stingy as that; but I want *you* to have them, and then when I get bigger they'll do for me—oh-h—count the pieces, Hans. Did ever you see so many!"

Hans turned the money thoughtfully in his palm. Never in all his life had he longed so intensely for a pair of skates, for he had known of the race and had, boy-like, fairly ached for a chance to test his powers with the other children. He felt confident that with a good pair of steel runners he could easily distance most of the boys on the canal. Then, too, Gretel's argument was so plausible. On the other hand, he knew that she, with her strong but lithe little frame, needed but a week's practice on good runners, to make her a better skater than Rychie van Korbes or even Katrinka Flack. As soon as this last thought flashed upon him his resolve was made. If Gretel would not have the jacket, she should have the skates.

"No, Gretel," he answered at last, "I can wait. Some day

I may have money enough saved to buy a fine pair. You shall have these."

Gretel's eyes sparkled, but in another instant she insisted, rather faintly:

"The young lady gave the money to *you,* Hans. I'd be real bad to take it."

Hans shook his head, resolutely, as he trudged on, causing his sister to half skip and half walk in her effort to keep beside him. By this time they had taken off their wooden "rockers" and were hastening home to tell their mother the good news.

"Oh! *I* know!" cried Gretel, in a sprightly tone. "You can do this. You can get a pair a little too small for you and too big for me, and we can take turns and use them. Won't that be fine?" and Gretel clapped her hands again.

Poor Hans! This was a strong temptation, but he pushed it away from him, brave-hearted fellow that he was.

"Nonsense, Gretel. You could never get on with a big pair. You stumbled about with these, like a blind chicken, before I curved off the ends. No, you must have a pair to fit exactly, and you must practice every chance you can get, until the twentieth comes. My little Gretel shall win the silver skates."

Gretel could not help laughing with delight at the very idea.

"Hans! Gretel!" called out a familiar voice.

"Coming, mother!" and they hastened toward the cottage, Hans still shaking the pieces of silver in his hand.

On the following day there was not a prouder nor a happier boy in all Holland than Hans Brinker, as he watched his sister, with many a dexterous sweep, flying in and out among the skaters who at sundown thronged the canal. A warm jacket had been given her by the kind-hearted Hilda, and the burst-out shoes had been cobbled into decency by Dame Brinker. As the little creature darted backward and forward, flushed with enjoyment, and quite unconscious of the many wondering glances bent upon her, she felt that the shining runners beneath her feet had suddenly turned earth into Fairyland, while "Hans, dear, good Hans!" echoed itself over and over again in her grateful heart.

"By den donder!" exclaimed Peter van Holp to Carl Schummel, "but that little one in the red jacket and patched petticoat skates well. Gunst! she has toes on her heels and eyes in the back of her head! See her! It will be a joke if she gets in the race and beats Katrinka Flack, after all."

"Hush! not so loud!" returned Carl, rather sneeringly. "That little lady in rags is the special pet of Hilda van Gleck. Those shining skates are her gift, if I make no mistake."

"So! so!" exclaimed Peter, with a radiant smile, for Hilda was his best friend. "She has been at her good work there, too!" And Mynheer van Holp, after cutting a double 8 on the ice, to say nothing of a huge P, then a jump, and an H, glided onward until he found himself beside Hilda.

Hand in hand they skated together, laughingly at first, then staidly talking in a low tone.

Strange to say, Peter van Holp soon arrived at a sudden conviction that his little sister needed a wooden chain just like Hilda's.

Two days afterward, on St. Nicholas' Eve, Hans, having burned three candle-ends, and cut his thumb into the bargain, stood in the market place at Amsterdam, buying another pair of skates.

IV

SHADOWS IN THE HOME

GOOD Dame Brinker! As soon as the scanty dinner had been cleared away that noon, she had arrayed herself in her holiday attire, in honor of Saint Nicholas. "It will brighten the children," she thought to herself, and she was not mistaken. This festival dress had been worn very seldom during the past ten years; before that time it had done good service, and had flourished at many a dance and Kermis, when she was known far and wide, as the pretty Meitje Klenck. The knitted woolen mitts, and the dainty cap showing her hair, which generally was hidden, made her seem almost like a princess to Gretel, while Master Hans grew staid and well-behaved as he gazed.

"Oh, mother, mother, mother, how **pretty you are!** Look, Hans! Isn't it just like a picture?"

27

"Just like a picture," assented Hans, cheerfully, "*just* like a picture—only I don't like those stocking things on the hands."

"Not like the mitts, brother Hans! Why, they're very important—see—they cover up all the red. Oh, mother, how white your arm is where the mitt leaves off, whiter than mine; oh, ever so much whiter. I declare, mother, the bodice is tight for you. You're growing! you're surely growing!"

Dame Brinker laughed.

"This was made long ago, lovey, when I wasn't much thicker about the waist than a churn-dasher. And how do you like the cap?" turning her head from side to side.

"Oh, *ever* so much, mother. It's b-e-a-u-t-i-f-u-l! See! the father is looking!"

Was the father looking? Alas, only with a dull stare. His vrouw turned toward him with a start, something like a blush rising to her cheeks, a questioning sparkle in her eye. The bright look died away in an instant.

"No, no," she sighed, "he sees nothing. Come, Hans" (and the smile crept faintly back again), "don't stand gaping at me all day, and the new skates waiting for you at Amsterdam."

"Ah, mother," he answered, "you need many things. Why should I buy skates?"

"Nonsense, child. The money was given to you on purpose, or the work was—it's all the same thing. Go, while the sun is high."

"Yes, and hurry back, Hans!" laughed Gretel, "we'll race on the canal tonight, if the mother lets us."

At the very threshold he turned to say—"Your spinning-wheel wants a new treadle, mother."

"You can make it, Hans."

"So I can. That will take no money. But you need feathers, and wool and meal, and—"

"There, there! That will do. Your silver cannot buy everything. Ah! Hans, if our stolen money would but come back on this bright Saint Nicholas' Eve, how glad we would be! Only last night I prayed to the good Saint—"

"Mother!" interrupted Hans in dismay.

"Why not, Hans! Shame on you to reproach me for that! I'm as true a Protestant, in sooth, as any fine lady that walks into church, but it's no wrong to turn sometimes to the good Saint Nicholas. Tut! It's a likely story if one can't do that, without one's children flaring up at it—and he the boys' and girls' own saint—Hoot! mayhap the colt is a steadier horse than the mare?"

Hans knew his mother too well to offer a word in opposition, when her voice quickened and sharpened, as it did now (it was often sharp and quick when she spoke of the missing money), so he said gently:

"And what did you ask of good Saint Nicholas, mother?"

"Why, to never give the thieves a wink of sleep till they brought it back, to be sure, if he's power to do such things, or else to brighten our wits that we might find it ourselves. Not a sight have I had of it since the day before the dear father was hurt—as you well know, Hans."

"That I do, mother," he answered sadly, "though you have almost pulled down the cottage in searching."

"Aye; but it was of no use," moaned the dame. "'Hiders make best finders.'"

Hans started. "Do you think the father could tell aught?" he asked mysteriously.

"Aye, indeed," said Dame Brinker, nodding her head, "I think so, but that is no sign. I never hold the same belief in the matter two days. Mayhap the father paid it off for the great silver watch we have been guarding since that day. But, no—I'll never believe it."

"The watch was not worth a quarter of the money, mother."

"No, indeed; and your father was a shrewd man up to the last moment. He was too steady and thrifty for silly doings."

"Where *did* the watch come from, I wonder?" muttered Hans, half to himself.

Dame Brinker shook her head and looked sadly toward her husband, who sat staring blankly at the floor. Gretel stood near him, knitting.

"That we shall never know, Hans. I have shown it to the father many a time, but he does not know it from a potato. When he came in that dreadful night to supper, he handed the watch to me and told me to take good care of it until he asked for it again. Just as he opened his lips to say more, Broom Klatterboost came flying in with word that the dyke was in danger. Ah! the waters were terrible that holy Pinxter-week! My man, alack! caught up his tools and ran out. That was the last I ever saw of him in his right mind. He was brought in again by midnight, nearly dead, with his poor head all bruised and cut. The fever passed off in time, but never the dullness— *that* grew worse every day. We shall never know."

Hans had heard all this before. More than once he had seen his mother, in hours of sore need, take the watch from its hiding-place, half-resolved to sell it, but she had always conquered the temptation.

"No, Hans," she would say, "we must be nearer starving than this before we turn faithless to the father!"

A memory of some such scene crossed her son's mind now; for, after giving a heavy sigh, and filliping a crumb of wax at Gretel across the table, he said:

"Aye, mother, you have done bravely to keep it—many a one would have tossed it off for gold long ago."

"And more shame for them!" exclaimed the dame, indignantly, "*I* would not do it. Besides, the gentry are so hard on us poor folks that if they saw such a thing in our hands, even if we told all, they might suspect the father of—"

Hans flushed angrily.

"They would not *dare* to say such a thing, mother! If they did—I'd—"

He clenched his fist and seemed to think that the rest of his sentence was too terrible to utter in her presence.

Dame Brinker smiled proudly through her tears at this interruption.

"Ah, Hans, thou'rt a true, brave lad. We will never part company with the watch. In his dying hour the dear father might wake and ask for it."

"Might *wake,* mother!" echoed Hans, "wake—and know us?"

"Aye, child," almost whispered his mother, "such things have been."

By this time Hans had nearly forgotten his proposed errand to Amsterdam. His mother had seldom spoken so familiarly with him. He felt himself now to be not only her son, but her friend, her adviser.

"You are right, mother. We must never give up the watch. For the father's sake, we will guard it always. The money, though, may come to light when we least expect it."

"Never!" cried Dame Brinker, taking the last stitch from her needle with a jerk, and laying the unfinished knitting heavily upon her lap. "There is no chance! One thousand guilders! and all gone in a day! One thousand guilders—Oh! what ever *did* become of them? If they went in an evil way, the thief would have confessed by this on his dying bed—he would not dare to die with such guilt on his soul!"

"He may not be dead yet," said Hans, soothingly, "any day we may hear of him."

"Ah, child," she said, in a changed tone, "what thief would ever have come *here?* It was always neat and clean, thank God! but not fine; for the father and I saved and saved that we might have something laid by. 'Little and often soon fills the pouch.' We found it so, in truth; besides, the father had a goodly sum, already, for service done to the Heernocht lands, at the time of the great inundation. Every week we had a guilder left over, sometimes more; for the father worked extra hours, and could get high pay for his labor. Every Saturday night we put something by, except the time when you had the fever, Hans, and when Gretel came. At last the pouch grew so full that I mended an old stocking and commenced again. Now that I look back, it seems that the money was up to the heel in a few sunny weeks. There was great pay in those days if a man was quick at engineer work. The stocking went on filling with copper and silver—aye, and gold. You may well open your eyes, Gretel. I used to laugh and tell the father it was not for poverty I wore my old gown;—and the stocking went on filling—so full that sometimes when I woke at night, I'd get up, soft and quiet, and go feel it in the moonlight. Then, on my knees, I would thank our Lord that my little ones could in time get good learning, and that the father might rest from labor in his old age. Sometimes, at supper, the father and I would talk about a new chimney and a good winter-room for the cow; but my man forsooth had finer plans even than that. 'A big sail,' says he, 'catches the wind—we can do what we will soon,' and then we would sing together as I washed my dishes. Ah, 'a smooth sea makes an easy rudder,'—not a thing vexed me from morning till night.

Every week the father would take out the stocking and drop in the money, and laugh and kiss me as we tied it up together.——— Up with you, Hans! there you sit gaping and the day a-wasting!" added Dame Brinker tartly, blushing to find that she had been speaking too freely to her boy, "it's high time you were on your way."

Hans had seated himself and was looking earnestly into her face. He arose and, in almost a whisper, asked:

"Have you ever *tried,* mother?"

She understood him.

"Yes, child, often. But the father only laughs, or he stares at me so strange I am glad to ask no more. When you and Gretel had the fever last winter and our bread was nearly gone, and I could earn nothing, for fear you would die while my face was turned, oh! I tried then! I smoothed his hair, and whispered to him soft as a kitten, about the money—where it was—who had it? Alack! he would pick at my sleeve, and whisper gibberish till my blood ran cold. At last, while Gretel lay whiter than snow, and you were raving on the bed, I SCREAMED to him—it seemed as if he *must* hear me—'Raff, where is our money? Do you know aught of the money, Raff?—the money in the pouch and the stocking, in the big chest?'—but I might as well have talked to a stone—I might as—"

The mother's voice sounded so strangely, and her eye was so bright, that Hans, with a new anxiety, laid his hand upon her shoulder.

"Come, mother," he said, "let us try to forget this money. I am big and strong—Gretel, too, is very quick and willing. Soon all will be prosperous with us again. Why, mother, Gretel and I would rather see thee bright and happy, than to have all the silver in the world—wouldn't we, Gretel?"

"The mother knows it," said Gretel, sobbing.

V

D AME BRINKER was startled at her children s emotion;
glad, too, for it proved how loving and true they were.

Beautiful ladies, in princely homes, often smile suddenly
and sweetly, gladdening the very air around them; but I doubt
if their smile be more welcome in God's sight than that which
sprang forth to cheer the roughly clad boy and girl in the
humble cottage. Dame Brinker felt that she had been selfish.
Blushing and brightening, she hastily wiped her eyes, and looked
upon them as only a mother can.

"Hoity! toity! Pretty talk we're having, and Sairt Nicholas' Eve almost here! What wonder the yarn pricks my fingers!
Come, Gretel, take this money, and while Hans is trading for
the skates you can buy a waffle in the market place."

"Let me stay home with you, mother," said Gretel, looking
up with eyes that sparkled through their tears. "Hans will buy
me the cake."

"As you will, child, and Hans—wait a moment. Three
turns of the needle will finish this toe, and then you may have
as good a pair of hose as ever were knitted (owning the yarn is
a grain too sharp), to sell to the hosier on the Heireen Gracht.
That will give us three quarter-guilders if you make good trade;
and as it's right hungry weather, you may buy four waffles.
We'll keep the Feast of Saint Nicholas after all."

Gretel clapped her hands. "That will be fine! Annie Bouman told me what grand times they will have in the big houses tonight. But we will be merry, too. Hans will have beautiful new skates—and then there'll be the waffles! Oh-h! Don't break them, brother Hans. Wrap them well, and button them under your jacket very carefully."

"Certainly," replied Hans, quite gruff with pleasure and importance."

"Oh! mother!" cried Gretel, in high glee, "soon you will be busied with the father, and now you are only knitting. Do tell us all about Saint Nicholas!"

Dame Brinker laughed to see Hans hang up his hat and prepare to listen. "Nonsense, children," she said, "I have told it to you often."

"Tell us again! oh, *do* tell us again!" cried Gretel, throwing herself upon the wonderful wooden bench that her brother had made on the mother's last birthday. Hans, not wishing to appear childish, and yet quite willing to hear the story, stood carelessly swinging his skates against the fireplace.

"Well, children, you shall hear it, but we must never waste the daylight again in this way. Pick up your ball, Gretel, and let your sock grow as I talk. Opening your ears needn't shut your fingers. Saint Nicholas, you must know, is a wonderful saint. He keeps his eye open for the good of sailors, but he cares most of all for boys and girls. Well, once upon a time, when he was living on the earth, a merchant of Asia sent his three sons to a great city, called Athens, to get learning."

"Is Athens in Holland, mother?" asked Gretel.

"I don't know, child. Probably it is.'

"Oh, no, mother," said Hans, respectfully. "I had that in my geography lessons long ago. Athens is in Greece."

"Well," resumed the mother, "what matter? Greece may belong to the King, for aught we know. Anyhow, this rich merchant sent his sons to Athens. While they were on their way they stopped one night at a shabby inn, meaning to take up their journey in the morning. Well, they had very fine clothes—velvet and silk, it may be, such as rich folks' children, all over the world, think nothing of wearing—and their belts, likewise, were full of money. What did the wicked landlord do, but contrive a plan to kill the children, and take their money and all their beautiful clothes himself. So that night, when all the world was asleep, he got up and killed the three young gentlemen."

Gretel clasped her hands and shuddered, but Hans tried to look as if killing and murder were every-day matters to him.

"That was not the worst of it," continued Dame Brinker, knitting slowly and trying to keep count of her stitches as she talked, "that was not near the worst of it. The dreadful landlord went and cut up the young gentlemen's bodies into little pieces and threw them into a great tub of brine, intending to sell them for pickled pork!"

"Oh!" cried Gretel, horror-stricken, though she had often heard the story before. Hans still continued unmoved and seemed to think that pickling was the best that could be done under the circumstances.

"Yes, he pickled them, and one might think that would have been the last of the young gentlemen. But no. That night Saint Nicholas had a wonderful vision, and in it he saw the landlord cutting up the merchant's children. There was no need of his hurrying, you know, for he was a saint; but in the morning he went to the inn and charged the landlord with the murder. Then the wicked landlord confessed it from beginning to end and fell down on his knees, begging forgiveness.

He felt so sorry for what he had done that he asked the saint to bring the young masters to life."

"And did the saint do it?" asked Gretel, delighted, well knowing what the answer would be.

"Of course he did. The pickled pieces flew together in an instant, and out jumped the young gentlemen from the brine-tub. They cast themselves at the feet of Saint Nicholas and he gave them his blessing, and—oh! mercy on us, Hans, it will be dark before you get back if you don't start this minute!"

By this time Dame Brinker was almost out of breath and quite out of commas. She could not remember when she had seen the children idle away an hour of daylight in this manner, and the thought of such luxury quite appalled her. By way of compensation she now flew about the room in extreme haste. Tossing a block of peat upon the fire, blowing invisible dust from the table, and handing the finished hose to Hans, all in an instant—

"Come, Hans," she said, as her boy lingered by the door, "what keeps thee?"

Hans kissed his mother's plump cheek, rosy and fresh yet, in spite of all her troubles—"my mother is the best in the world, and I would be right glad to have a pair of skates, but"—and, as he buttoned his jacket, he looked, in a troubled way, toward a strange figure crouching by the hearthstone—"if my money would bring a meester* from Amsterdam to see the father, something might yet be done."

"A meester would not come, Hans, for twice that money; and it would do no good if he did. Ah! how many guilders I once spent for that; but the dear, good father would not waken. It is God's will. Go, Hans, and buy the skates."

* Doctor (dokter in Dutch) called meester by the lower class.

Hans started with a heavy heart, but since the heart was young, and in the boy's bosom, it set him whistling in less than five minutes. His mother had said "thee" to him, and that was quite enough to make even a dark day sunny. Hollanders do not address each other in affectionate intercourse, as the French and Germans do. But Dame Brinker had embroidered for a Heidelberg family in her girlhood, and she had carried its "thee" and "thou" into her rude home, to be used in moments of extreme love and tenderness.

Therefore, "What keeps thee, Hans?" sang an echo song beneath the boy's whistling and made him feel that his errand was blest.

VI

HANS HAS HIS WAY

BROEK, with its quiet, spotless streets, its frozen rivulets, its yellow brick pavements, and bright wooden houses, was near by. It was a village where neatness and show were in full blossom; but the inhabitants seemed to be either asleep or dead.

Not a footprint marred the sanded paths, where pebbles and seashells lay in fanciful designs. Every window shutter was closed as tightly as though air and sunshine were poison; and the massive front doors were never opened except on the occasion of a wedding, christening, or a funeral.

Hans glanced toward the village, as he shook his silver pieces, and wondered whether it were really true, as he had often heard, that some of the people of Broek were so rich that they used kitchen utensils of solid gold.

He had seen Mevrouw van Stoop's cheeses in market, and he knew that the lofty dame earned many a bright silver guilder in selling them. But did she set the cream to rise in golden pans? Did she use a golden skimmer? When her cows were in winter quarters, were their tails really tied up with ribbons?

These thoughts ran through his mind as he turned his

face toward Amsterdam, not five miles away, on the other side of the frozen Y. The ice upon the canal was perfect, but his wooden runners, so soon to be cast aside, squeaked a dismal farewell, as he scraped and skimmed along.

When crossing the Y, whom should he see skating toward him but the great Dr. Boekman, the most famous physician and surgeon in Holland. Hans had never met him before, but he had seen his engraved likeness in many of the shop windows in Amsterdam. It was a face that one could never forget. Thin and lank, though a born Dutchman, with stern blue eyes, and queer, compressed lips, that seemed to say, "No smiling permitted," he certainly was not a very jolly or sociable looking personage, nor one that a well-trained boy would care to accost unbidden.

But Hans *was* bidden, and that, too, by a voice he seldom disregarded—his own conscience.

"Here comes the greatest doctor in the world," whispered the voice, "God has sent him; you have no right to buy skates when you might, with the same money, purchase such aid for your father!"

The wooden runners gave an exultant squeak. Hundreds of beautiful skates were gleaming and vanishing in the air above him. He felt the money tingle in his fingers. The old doctor looked fearfully grim and forbidding. Hans' heart was in his throat, but he found voice enough to cry out, just as he was passing:

"Mynheer Boekman!"

The great man halted and, sticking out his thin under lip, looked scowlingly about him.

Hans was in for it now.

"Mynheer," he panted, drawing close to the fierce-looking

doctor, "I knew you could be none other than the famous Boekman. I have to ask a great favor—"

"Humph!" muttered the doctor, preparing to skate past the intruder—"Get out of the way—I've no money—never give to beggars."

"I am no beggar, Mynheer," retorted Hans proudly, at the same time producing his mite of silver with a grand air, "I wish to consult with you about my father. He is a living man, but sits like one dead. He cannot think. His words mean nothing—but he is not sick. He fell on the dykes."

"Hey? what?" cried the doctor, beginning to listen.

Hans told the whole story in an incoherent way, dashing off a tear once or twice as he talked, and finally ending with an earnest,

"Oh, do see him, Mynheer. His body is well—it is only his mind—I know this money is not enough; but take it, Mynheer, I will earn more—I know I will—Oh! I will toil for you all my life, if you will but cure my father!"

What was the matter with the old doctor? A brightness like sunlight beamed from his face. His eyes were kind and moist; the hand that had lately clutched his cane as if preparing to strike, was laid gently upon Hans' shoulder.

"Put up your money, boy, I do not want it—we will see your father. It is a hopeless case, I fear. How long did you say?"

"Ten years, Mynheer," sobbed Hans, radiant with sudden hope.

"Ah! a bad case; but I shall see him. Let me think. To-day I start for Leyden, to return in a week, then you may expect me. Where is it?"

"A mile south of Broek, Mynheer, near the canal. It is

only a poor, broken-down hut. Any of the children thereabout can point it out to your honor," added Hans, with a heavy sigh; "they are all half afraid of the place; they call it the idiot's cottage."

"That will do," said the doctor, hurrying on, with a bright backward nod at Hans, "I shall be there. A hopeless case," he muttered to himself, "but the boy pleases me. His eye is like my poor Laurens'. Confound it, shall I never forget that young scoundrel!" and, scowling more darkly than ever, the doctor pursued his silent way.

Again Hans was skating toward Amsterdam on the squeaking wooden runners; again his fingers tingled against the money in his pocket; again the boyish whistle rose unconsciously to his lips:

"Shall I hurry home," he was thinking, "to tell the good news, or shall I get the waffles and the new skates first? Whew! I think I'll go on!"

And so Hans bought the skates.

VII

HANS and Gretel had a fine frolic early on that Saint Nicholas' Eve. There was a bright moon, and their mother, though she believed herself to be without any hope of her husband's improvement, had been made so happy at the prospect of the meester's visit that she had yielded to the children's entreaties for an hour's skating before bedtime.

Hans was delighted with his new skates, and in his eagerness to show Gretel how perfectly they "worked," did many things upon the ice that caused the little maid to clasp her hands in solemn admiration. They were not alone, though they seemed quite unheeded by the various groups assembled upon the canal.

The two Van Holps and Carl Schummel were there, testing their fleetness to the utmost. Out of four trials Peter van Holp had beaten three times. Consequently Carl, never very amiable, was in anything but a good humor. He had relieved himself by taunting young Schimmelpenninck, who, being smaller than the others, kept meekly near them, without feeling exactly like one of the party; but now a new thought seized Carl, or rather he seized the new thought and made an onset upon his friends.

"I say, boys, let's put a stop to those young rag-pickers from the idiot's cottage joining the race. Hilda must be crazy to think of it. Katrinka Flack and Rychie van Korbes are furious at the very idea of racing with the girl; and for my part, I don't blame them. As for the boy, if we've a spark of manhood in us we will scorn the very idea of—"

"Certainly we will!" interposed Peter van Holp, purposely mistaking Carl's meaning, "who doubts it? No fellow with a spark of manhood in him would refuse to let in two good skaters just because they were poor!"

Carl wheeled about savagely—

"Not so fast, master! and I'd thank you not to put words in other people's mouths. You'd best not try it again."

"Ha! ha!" laughed little Voostenwalbert Schimmelpenninck, delighted at the prospect of a fight, and sure that, if it should come to blows, his favorite, Peter, could beat a dozen excitable fellows like Carl.

Something in Peter's eye made Carl glad to turn to a weaker offender. He wheeled furiously upon Voost.

"What are you shrieking about, you little weasel! You skinny herring, you; you little monkey with a long name for a tail!"

Half-a-dozen by-standers and by-skaters set up an applauding shout at this brave witticism; and Carl, feeling that he had fairly vanquished his foes, was restored to partial good humor. He, however, prudently resolved to defer plotting against Hans and Gretel until some time when Peter should not be present.

Just then his friend, Jacob Poot, was seen approaching. They could not distinguish his features at first; but as he was the stoutest boy in the neighborhood there could be no mistaking his form.

"Hello! here comes Fatty!" exclaimed Carl, "and there's some one with him, a slender fellow, a stranger."

"Ha! ha! that's like good bacon," cried Ludwig; "a streak of lean and a streak of fat."

"That's Jacob's English cousin," put in Master Voost, delighted at being able to give the information, "that's his English cousin, and, oh! he's got such a funny little name— *Ben Dobbs.* He's going to stay with him until after the grand race."

All this time the boys had been spinning, turning, "rolling," and doing other feats upon their skates, in a quiet way, as they talked; but now they stood still, bracing themselves against the frosty air as Jacob Poot and his friend drew near.

"This is my cousin, boys," said Jacob, rather out of breath—"Benjamin Dobbs. He's a John Bull and he's going to be in the race."

Master Dobbs felt at first very awkward among his cousin's friends. Though most of them had studied English and French, they were shy about attempting to speak either, and he made very funny blunders when he tried to converse in Dutch.

However, the fun of skating glides over all barriers of speech. Through this, Ben soon felt that he knew the boys well, and when Jacob (with a sprinkling of French and English for Ben's benefit), told of a grand project they had planned, his cousin could now and then put in a "ja," or a nod, in quite a familiar way.

The project *was* a grand one and there was to be a fine opportunity for carrying it out; for, besides the allotted holiday of the Festival of Saint Nicholas, four extra days were to be allowed for a general cleaning of the school-house.

Jacob and Ben had obtained permission to go on a long skating journey—no less a one than from Broek to The Hague, the capital of Holland, a distance of nearly fifty miles!

"And now, boys," added Jacob, when he had told the plan, "who will go with us?"

"I will! I will!" cried the boys eagerly.

"And so will I!" ventured little Voostenwalbert.

"Ha! ha!" laughed Jacob, holding his fat sides and shaking his puffy cheeks, *"you* go? Such a little fellow as you? Why, youngster, you haven't left off your pads yet!"

Now in Holland very young children wear a thin, padded cushion around their heads, surmounted with a framework of whalebone and ribbon, to protect them in case of a fall; and it is the dividing line between babyhood and childhood when they leave it off. Voost had arrived at this dignity several years before, consequently Jacob's insult was rather too great for endurance.

"Look out what you say!" he squeaked. "Lucky for you when you can leave off *your* pads—you're padded all over!"

"Ha! ha!" roared all the boys except Master Dobbs, who could not understand. "Ha! ha!"—and the good-natured Jacob laughed more than any.

"It ish my fat—he say I bees pad mit fat!" he explained to Ben.

So a vote was passed unanimously in favor of allowing the now popular Voost to join the party, if his parents would consent.

"Good-night!" sang out the happy youngster, skating homeward with all his might.

"Good-night."

"We can stop at Haarlem, Jacob, and show your cousin the big organ," said Peter van Holp, eagerly, "and at Leyden, too, where there's no end to the sights; and spend a day and night at The Hague, for my married sister, who lives there, will be delighted to see us; and the next morning we can start for home."

"All right!" responded Jacob, who was not much of a talker.

Ludwig had been regarding his brother with enthusiastic admiration.

"Hurrah for you, Pete! It takes you to make plans! Mother'll be as full of it as we are when we tell her we can take her love direct to sister Van Gend. My! but it's cold," he added, "cold enough to take a fellow's head off his shoulders. We'd better go home."

"What if it is cold, old Tender-skin?" cried Carl, who was busily practicing a step which he called the "double edge." "Great skating we should have by this time, if it was as warm as it was last December. Don't you know, if it wasn't an extra cold winter, and an early one into the bargain, we couldn't go?"

"I know it's an extra cold night, anyhow," said Ludwig. "Whew! I'm going home!"

"Good-night!" cried one and all, and off they started, shouting, singing and laughing as they flew along.

Where were Gretel and Hans?

They had skated about an hour, keeping aloof from the others—quite contented with each other, and Gretel had exclaimed, "Ah, Hans, how beautiful! how fine! To think that we both have skates! I tell you, the stork brought us good luck!"—when they heard something!

It was a scream—a very faint scream! No one else upon the canal observed it, but Hans knew its meaning too well. Gretel saw him turn white in the moonlight as he hastily tore off his skates.

"The father!" he cried, "he has frightened our mother!" and Gretel ran after him toward the house as rapidly as she could.

VIII

THE FESTIVAL OF SAINT NICHOLAS

WE all know how, before the Christmas tree began to flourish in the home-life of our country, a certain "right jolly old elf," with "eight tiny reindeer," used to drive his sleigh-load of toys up to our house-tops and then bound down the chimney to fill the stockings so hopefully hung by the fireplace. His friends called him Santa Claus, and those who were most intimate ventured to say "Old Nick." It was said that he originally came from Holland. Doubtless he did; but, if so, he certainly, like many other foreigners, changed his ways very much after landing upon our shores. In Holland, Saint Nicholas is a veritable saint, and often appears in full costume, with his embroidered robes, glittering with gems and gold, his mitre, his crozier and his jeweled gloves. *Here* Santa Claus comes rollicking along, on the twenty-fifth of December, our holy Christmas morn. But in Holland, Saint Nicholas visits earth on the fifth, a time especially appropriated to him. Early on the morning of the sixth, he distributes his candies, toys and treasures, and vanishes for a year.

Christmas day is devoted by the Hollanders to church rites and pleasant family visiting. It is on Saint Nicholas' Eve that their young people become half wild with joy and expectation. To some of them it is a sorry time, for the saint is very candid, and if any of them have been bad during the past year, he is quite sure to tell them so. Sometimes he carries a birch rod under his arm and advises the parents to give them scoldings in place of confections and floggings instead of toys.

It was well that the boys hastened to their abodes on that bright winter evening, for in less than an hour afterwards the saint made his appearance in half the homes of Holland.

Hilda van Gleck's little brothers and sisters were in a high state of excitement that night. They had been admitted into the grand parlor; they were dressed in their best, and had been given two cakes apiece at supper. Hilda was as joyous as any. Why not? Saint Nicholas would never cross a girl of fourteen from his list, just because she was tall and looked almost like a woman. On the contrary, he would probably exert himself to do honor to such an august-looking damsel. Who could tell? So she sported and laughed and danced as gaily as the youngest, and was the soul of all their merry games. At last matters grew so uproarious that Mynheer van Gleck regarded his children with astonishment. The baby even showed symptoms of hysterics. It was high time to attend to business. Madame suggested that if they wished to see the good Saint Nicholas they should sing the same loving invitation that had brought him the year before.

The baby stared and thrust his fist into his mouth as mynheer put him down upon the floor. Soon he sat erect and looked with a sweet scowl at the company.

The other children, each holding a pretty willow basket, formed at once in a ring, and moved slowly around the little fellow, lifting their eyes, meanwhile, for the saint to whom they were about to address themselves was yet in mysterious quarters.

Madame commenced playing softly upon the piano; soon the voices rose—gentle, youthful voices—rendered all the sweeter for their tremor:

"Welcome, friend! Saint Nicholas, welcome!
Bring no rod for us, tonight!
While our voices bid thee welcome,
Every heart with joy is light!

"Tell us every fault and failing,
We will bear thy keenest railing,
So we sing—so we sing—
Will you bring us anything?

"Welcome, friend! Saint Nicholas, welcome!
Welcome to this merry band!
Happy children greet thee, welcome!
Thou art glad'ning all the land!

"Fill each empty hand and basket,
'Tis thy little ones who ask it.
So we sing—so we sing—
Thou wilt bring us everything!"

During the chorus, sundry glances, half in eagerness, half in dread, had been cast towards the polished folding doors. Now a loud knocking was heard. The circle was broken in an instant. Some of the little ones, with a strange mixture of fear and delight, pressed against their mother's knee.

"Come in," said Madame, softly.

The door slowly opened and Saint Nicholas, in full array, stood before them. You could have heard a pin drop! Soon he spoke. What a mysterious majesty in his voice! what kindliness in his tones!

"Karel van Gleck, I am pleased to greet thee, and thy honored vrouw Kathrine, and thy son and his good vrouw Annie!

"Children, I greet ye all! Hendrick, Hilda, Broom, Katy, Huygens, and Lucretia! And thy cousins, Wolfert, Diedrich, Mayken, Voost, and Katrina! Good children ye have been, in the main, since I last accosted ye. Diedrich was rude at the Haarlem fair last fall, but he has tried to atone for it since. Mayken has failed of late in her lessons, and too many

THE DOOR SLOWLY OPENED AND SAINT NICHOLAS, IN FULL
ARRAY, STOOD BEFORE THEM.

sweets and trifles have gone to her lips, and too few dimes to her charity-box. Diedrich, I trust, will be a polite, manly boy for the future, and Mayken will endeavor to shine as a student. Let her remember, too, that economy and thrift are needed in the foundation of a worthy and generous life. Little Katy has been cruel to the cat more than once. Saint Nicholas can hear the cat cry when its tail is pulled. I will forgive her if she will remember from this hour that the smallest dumb creatures have feelings and must not be abused."

As Katy burst into a frightened cry, the saint graciously remained silent until she was soothed.

"Master Broom," he resumed, "I warn thee that boys who are in the habit of putting snuff upon the foot-stove of the schoolmistress may one day be discovered and receive a flogging—"

[Master Broom colored and stared in great astonishment.]

"But thou art such an excellent scholar, I shall make thee no further reproof.

"Thou, Hendrick, didst distinguish thyself in the archery match last spring and hit the bull's-eye, though the bird was swung before it to unsteady thine eye. I give thee credit for excelling in manly sport and exercise—though I must not unduly countenance thy boat-racing, since it leaves thee too little time for thy proper studies.

"Lucretia and Hilda shall have a blessed sleep tonight. The consciousness of kindness to the poor, devotion in their souls, and cheerful, hearty obedience to household rule will render them happy.

"With one and all I avow myself well content. Goodness, industry, benevolence and thrift have prevailed in your midst. Therefore, my blessing upon you—and may the New Year find all treading the paths of obedience, wisdom and love.

Tomorrow you shall find more substantial proofs that I have been in your midst. Farewell!"

With these words came a great shower of sugar-plums, upon a linen sheet spread out in front of the doors. A general scramble followed. The children fairly tumbled over each other in their eagerness to fill their baskets. Madame cautiously held the baby down in their midst, till the chubby little fists were filled. Then the bravest of the youngsters sprang up and burst open the closed doors—in vain they peered into the mysterious apartment—Saint Nicholas was nowhere to be seen.

Soon there was a general rush to another room, where stood a table, covered with the finest and whitest of linen damask. Each child, in a flutter of excitement, laid a shoe upon it. The door was then carefully locked and its key hidden in the mother's bedroom. Next followed good-night kisses, a grand family procession to the upper floor, merry farewells at bedroom doors—and silence, at last, reigned in the Van Gleck mansion

---

Early the next morning the door was solemnly unlocked and opened in the presence of the assembled household, when, lo! a sight appeared proving Saint Nicholas to be a saint of his word!

Every shoe was filled to overflowing and beside each stood many a colored pile. The table was heavy with its load of presents—candies, toys, trinkets, books and other articles. Every one had gifts, from grandfather down to the baby.

Little Katy clapped her hands with glee and vowed, inwardly, that the cat should never know another moment's grief.

Hendrick capered about the room, flourishing a superb bow and arrows over his head. Hilda laughed with delight as she opened a crimson box and drew forth its glittering contents. The rest chuckled and said "Oh!" and "Ah!" over their treasures, very much as we did here in America on last Christmas day.

With her glittering necklace in her hands and a pile of books in her arms, Hilda stole towards her parents and held up her beaming face for a kiss. There was such an earnest, tender look in her bright eyes that her mother breathed a blessing as she leaned over her.

"I am delighted with this book, thank you, father," she said, touching the top one with her chin. "I shall read it all day long."

Frolic and joy reigned supreme. A grand chorus of barking dogs, squeaking cats and bleating lambs, to say nothing of a noisy ivory cricket, that the baby was whirling with infinite delight, rose triumphant.

Good Saint Nicholas! For the sake of the young Hollanders, I, for one, am willing to acknowledge him, and defend his reality against all unbelievers.

Carl Schummel was quite busy during that day, assuring little children confidentially, that not Saint Nicholas, but their own fathers and mothers had produced the oracle and loaded the tables. But *we* know better than that.

And yet, if this were a saint, why did he not visit the Brinker cottage that night? Why was that one home, so dark and sorrowful, pased by?

IX

WHAT THE BOYS SAW AND DID IN AMSTERDAM

"ARE we all here?" cried Peter, in high glee, as the party assembled upon the canal early the next morning, equipped for their skating journey. "Let me see. As Jacob has made me captain, I must call the roll. Carl Schummel—. You here?"

"Ya!"

"Jacob Poot!"

"Ya!"

"Benjamin Dobbs!"

"Ya-a!"

"Lambert van Mounen!"

"Ya!"

"[That's lucky. Couldn't get on without *you,* as you're the only one who can speak English.] Ludwig van Holp!"

"Ya!"

"Voostenwalbert Schimmelpenninck!"

No answer.

"Ah! the little rogue has been kept at home. Now, boys, it's just eight o'clock—glorious weather, and the Y is as firm as a rock—we'll be at Amsterdam in thirty minutes. One, two, three, *start!*"

True enough, in less than half an hour they had crossed a dyke of solid masonry and were in the very heart of the great metropolis of the Netherlands—a walled city of ninety-five islands and nearly two hundred bridges. Although Ben had been twice there since his arrival in Holland, he saw much to excite wonder; but his Dutch comrades, having lived near by all their lives, considered it the most matter-of-course place in the world. Everything interested Ben; the tall houses with their forked chimneys; the narrow streets; the canals everywhere crossing the city; the bridges; the various costumes, and, strangest of all, shops and dwellings crouching close to the fronts of the churches.

Sometimes a dog-cart, heaped with wooden ware, passed him; then a donkey bearing a pair of panniers filled with crockery or glass; then a sled driven over the bare cobble-stones (the runners kept greased with a dripping oil rag, so that it might run easily); and then, perhaps, a showy but clumsy family carriage, drawn by the brownest of Flanders horses, swinging the whitest of snowy tails.

The city was in full festival array. Every shop was gorgeous in honor of Saint Nicholas. Captain Peter was forced, more than once, to order his men away from the tempting show windows, where everything that is, has been, or can be thought of in the way of toys was displayed. Tiny canal boats a foot long, and fitted out, complete, made his heart ache, he so longed to buy one at once for his little brother in England. He had no money to spare, for with true Dutch prudence, the party had agreed to take with them merely the sum required for each boy's expenses, and to consign the purse to Peter for safe-keeping. Consequently Master Ben concluded to devote all his energies to sight-seeing and to think as seldom as possible of little Robby.

The party skimmed along lightly upon the crowded canals. Lambert was busy pointing out things of interest to Ben, when he suddenly exclaimed: "Hello! the others are way ahead of us—all but Jacob. Whew! how fat he is! He'll break down before we're half-way."

Ben, of course, enjoyed skating beside Lambert, who, though a staunch Hollander, had been educated near London, and could speak English as fluently as Dutch; but he was not sorry when Captain van Holp called out:

"Skates off! There's the Museum!"

It was open and there was no charge on that day for admission. In they went, shuffling, as boys will, when they have a chance, just to hear the sound of their shoes on the polished floor.

This Museum is in fact a picture gallery where some of the finest works of the Dutch masters are to be seen, besides nearly two hundred portfolios of rare engravings.

"Boys!" called Lambert in a loud whisper, "come, look at this 'Bear Hunt'."

It was a fine painting by Paul Potter, a Dutch artist of the seventeenth century, who produced excellent works before he was sixteen years old. The boys admired it because the subject pleased them. They passed carelessly by the master-

pieces of Rembrandt and Van der Helst, and went into rap-
tures over an ugly picture by Van der Venne, representing a
sea-fight between the Dutch and English. They also stood
spellbound before a painting of two urchins, one of whom was
taking soup and the other eating an egg. The principal merit
in this work was that the young egg-eater had kindly slobbered
his face with the yolk for their entertainment.

"Come, boys!" cried the captain, "ten o'clock, time we
were off!"

They hastened to the canal.

"Skates on! Are you ready? *One, two*—hello! where's
Poot?"

Sure enough, where *was* Poot?

A square opening had just been cut in the ice not ten
yards off. Peter observed it and, without a word, skated rapidly toward it.

All the others followed, of course.

Peter looked in. They all looked in, then stared anxiously
at each other.

"Poot!" screamed Peter, peering into the hole again. All
was still. The black water gave no sign; it was already
glazing on top.

Van Mounen turned mysteriously to Ben.

"Didn't he have a fit once?"

"My goodness! yes!" answered Ben, in a great fright.

"Then, depend upon it, he's been taken with one in the
Museum!"

The boys caught his meaning. Every skate was off in a
twinkling. Peter had the presence of mind to scoop up a
capful of water from the hole, and off they scampered to the
rescue.

Alas! They did indeed find poor Jacob in a fit—but it was a fit of sleepiness. There he lay in a recess of the gallery, snoring like a trooper! The chorus of laughter that followed this discovery brought an angry official to the spot.

"What now! None of this racket! Here, you beer barrel, wake up!" and Master Jacob received a very unceremonious shaking.

As soon as Peter saw that Jacob's condition was not serious, he hastened to the street to empty his unfortunate cap. While he was stuffing in his handkerchief to prevent the already frozen crown from touching his head, the rest of the boys came down, dragging the bewildered and indignant Jacob in their midst.

The order to start was again given. Master Poot was wide awake at last. The ice was a little rough and broken just there, but every boy was in high spirits.

"Shall we go on by the canal or the river?" asked Peter.

"Oh, the river, by all means," said Carl. "It will be such fun; they say it is perfect skating all the way, but it's much farther."

Jacob Poot instantly became interested.

"I vote for the canal!" he cried.

"Well, the canal it shall be," responded the captain, "if all are agreed."

"Agreed!" they echoed, in rather a disappointed tone— and Captain Peter led the way.

"All right—come on—we can reach Haarlem in an hour!"

X

BIG MANIAS AND LITTLE ODDITIES

WHILE skating along at full speed, they heard the cars from Amsterdam coming close behind them.

"Hello!" cried Ludwig, glancing toward the rail-track—"who can't beat a locomotive? Let's give it a race!"

The whistle screamed at the very idea—so did the boys—and at it they went.

For an instant the boys were ahead, hurrahing with all their might,—only for an instant, but even *that* was something.

Nothing could be straighter than the canal upon which our party were skating, and nothing straighter than the long rows of willow trees that stood, bare and wispy, along the bank. Ben was in ecstacy with the scene.

Ludwig van Holp suddenly thought of something that he believed would make Ben open his eyes; he drew near Lambert with a triumphant:

"Tell him about the tulips!"

Ben caught the word "*tulpen.*"

"Oh! yes," said he eagerly, in English, "the Tulip Mania—are you speaking of that? I have often heard it mentioned, but know very little about it. It reached its height in Amsterdam, didn't it?"

"Yes, here and in Haarlem, principally; but the excitement ran high all over Holland, and in England, too, for that matter," replied Lambert.

"The first tulip was sent here from Constantinople about the year 1560. It was so much admired that the rich people of Amsterdam sent to Turkey for more. From that time they grew to be the rage.

"Everyone speculated in tulips, even the barge-men and rag-women, and chimney-sweeps. The richest merchants were not ashamed to share the excitement. People bought bulbs and sold them again at a tremendous profit without ever seeing them. It grew into a kind of gambling. Some became rich by it in a few days, and some lost everything they had. Land, houses, cattle, and even clothing went for tulips when people had no ready money. Ladies sold their jewels and finery to enable them to join in the fun. Nothing else was thought of. At last the states-general interfered. People began to see what geese they were making of themselves, and down went the price of tulips. Old tulip debts couldn't be collected. Creditors went to law and the law turned its back upon them; debts made in gambling were not binding, it said. Then there was a time! Thousands of rich speculators reduced to beggary in an hour. As old Beckman says, 'The bubble was burst at last.'"

"Yes, and a big bubble it was," said Ben, who had listened with great interest. "By the way, did you know that the name tulip came from a Turkish word, signifying 'turban'?"

"I had forgotten that," answered Lambert, "but it's a capital idea. Just fancy a party of Turks in full headgear, squatted upon a lawn—perfect tulip bed! Ha! ha! capital idea!"

The skaters glided along merrily. Finally Ben said: "If we were not exercising all the time we would freeze outright."

Lambert laughed.

"That's your English blood, Benjamin; *I'm* not cold.
And look at the skaters here on the canal—they're red as
roses, and happy as lords.   Hello! good Captain van Holp,"
called out Lambert in Dutch, "what say you to stopping at
yonder farm-house and warming our toes?"

"Who is cold?" asked Peter, turning around.

"Benjamin Dobbs."

"Benjamin Dobbs shall be warmed," and the party was
brought to a halt.

XI

A CATASTROPHE

ON approaching the door of the farm-house the boys suddenly found themselves in the midst of a lively domestic scene. A burly Dutchman came rushing out, closely followed by his dear *vrouw,* and she was beating him smartly with a long-handled warming-pan. The expression on her face gave our boys so little promise of a kind reception that they prudently resolved to carry their toes elsewhere to be warmed.

The next cottage proved to be more inviting. A neat, peaceful-looking old woman sat at one window, knitting. At the other could be discerned part of the profile of a fat figure that, pipe in mouth, sat behind the shining little panes and snowy curtain. In answer to Peter's subdued knock, a fair-haired, rosy-cheeked lass in holiday attire opened the upper half of the green door (which was divided across the middle) and inquired their errand.

"May we enter and warm ourselves, jufvrouw?" asked the captain respectfully.

"Yes, and welcome," was the reply, as the lower half of the door swung softly toward its mate. Every boy before entering rubbed long and faithfully upon the rough mat, and each made his best bow to the old lady and gentleman at the windows. They both nodded their heads slowly, in precisely

A BURLY DUTCHMAN CAME RUSHING OUT, CLOSELY FOLLOWED
BY HIS DEAR VROUW.

the same way, and both went on with their employment steadily and stiffly as though they worked by machinery.

But the rosy-cheeked maiden! Ah! how she bustled about. How she gave the boys polished, high-backed chairs to sit upon; she made Jacob Poot almost weep for joy by bringing forth a great square of gingerbread, and a stone jug of sour wine! How she laughed and nodded as the boys ate like wild animals on good behavior, and how blank she looked when Ben politely but firmly refused to take any black bread and sourkrout! How she pulled off Jacob's mitten, which was torn at the thumb, and mended it before his eyes, biting off the thread with her white teeth and saying, "Now it will be warmer," as she bit; and finally, how she shook hands with every boy in turn and insisted upon filling their pockets with gingerbread!

It was nearly one o'clock when Captain van Holp and his command entered the grand old city of Haarlem. They had skated nearly seventeen miles since morning and were still as fresh as young eagles. From the youngest (Ludwig van Holp, who was just fourteen) to the eldest, no less a personage than the captain himself, a veteran of seventeen, there was but one opinion—that this was the greatest frolic of their lives. Even Carl Schummel, who had become very intimate with Ludwig during the excursion, forgot to be ill-natured. As for Peter, he was the happiest of the happy, and had sung and whistled so joyously while skating that the staidest passers-by had smiled as they listened.

"Come, boys! it's nearly lunch hour," said Peter, as they neared a coffee-house on the main street. "We must have something more solid than the pretty maiden's gingerbread—"

and the captain plunged his hands into his pockets as if to say, "There's money enough here to feed an army!"

"Hello!" cried Lambert, "what ails the man?"

Peter, pale and staring, was clapping his hands upon his breast and sides—he looked like one suddenly becoming deranged.

"He's sick!" cried Ben.

"No, he's lost something," said Carl.

Peter could only gasp—"The pocketbook! with all our money in it—it's gone!"

For an instant all were too much startled to speak.

Carl at last came out with a gruff:

"No sense in letting one fellow have all the money. I said so from the first. Look in your other pocket."

"I did—it isn't there."

"Open your under jacket—"

Peter obeyed mechanically. He even took off his hat and looked into it—then thrust his hand desperately into every pocket."

"It's gone, boys," he said at last, in a hopeless tone. "No lunch for us, nor dinner either. What is to be done? We can't get on without money. If we were in Amsterdam I could get as much as we want, but there is not a man in Haarlem from whom I can borrow a dollar. Don't one of you know anyone here who would lend us a few guilders?"

Each boy looked into five blank faces. Then something like a smile passed around the circle, but it got sadly knotted up when it reached Carl.

"That wouldn't do," he said crossly, "I know some people here—rich ones, too—but father would flog me soundly if I borrowed a cent from anyone. He has *An honest man need not borrow* written over the gateway of his summer-house."

"Humph!" responded Peter, not particularly admiring the sentiment just at that moment

The boys grew desperately hungry at once.

"How much money have we lost?" asked Ludwig, dismally.

"Don't you remember," said Peter. "We each put in exactly ten guilders. The purse had sixty guilders in it. I am the stupidest fellow in the world; little Schimmelpenninck would have made you a better captain. I could pommel myself for bringing such a disappointment upon you."

"Do it then," growled Carl. "Pooh!" he added, "we all know it was an accident, but that doesn't help matters. We must have some money, Van Holp—even if you have to sell your wonderful watch."

"Sell my mother's birthday present! Never! I will sell my coat, my hat, anything but my watch."

"Come, come," said Jacob pleasantly, "we are making too much of this affair. We can go home and start again in a day or two."

"*You* may be able to get another ten-guilder piece," said Carl, "but the rest of us will not find it so easy. If we go home, we stay home, you may depend."

Our captain, whose good-nature had not yet forsaken him for a moment, grew indignant.

"Do you think I will let you suffer for my carelessness?" he exclaimed, "I have three times sixty guilders in my strong box at home!"

"Oh, I beg your pardon," said Carl hastily, adding, in a surlier tone: "Well, I see no better way than to go back hungry."

"I see a better plan than that," said the captain.

"What is it?" cried all the boys.

"Why, to make the best of a bad business and go back pleasantly, and like men," said Peter, looking so gallant and handsome as he turned his frank face and clear blue eyes upon them, that they caught his spirit.

"Ho for the Captain!" they shouted.

"Now, boys, we may as well make up our minds there's no place like Broek, after all—and that we mean to be there in two hours—is that agreed to?"

"Agreed!" cried all, as they ran to the canal.

"On with your skates! Are you ready? Here, Jacob, let me help you."

"Now. One, two, three—start!"

And the boyish faces that left Haarlem at that signal were nearly as bright as those that had entered it with Captain Peter half an hour before.

XII

HANS

"**D**ONDER and Blixin!" cried Carl angrily, before the party had skated twenty yards from the city gates, "if here isn't that wooden-skate ragamuffin in the patched leather breeches. That fellow is everywhere, confound him! We'll be lucky," he added, in as sneering a tone as he dared to assume, "if our captain doesn't order us to halt and shake hands with him."

"Your captain is a terrible fellow," said Peter, pleasantly, "but this is a false alarm, Carl—I cannot spy your bugbear anywhere among the skaters—ah! there he is! Why, what is the matter with the lad?"

Poor Hans! His face was pale, his lips compressed. He

skated like one under the effects of a fearful dream. Just as he was passing, Peter hailed him:

"Good-day, Hans Brinker!"

Hans' countenance brightened at once.—"Ah! mynheer, is that you? It is well we meet!"

"Just like his impertinence," hissed Carl Schummel, darting scornfully past his companions, who seemed inclined to linger with their captain.

"I am glad to see you, Hans," responded Peter, cheerily, "but you look troubled. Can I serve you?"

"I have a trouble, mynheer," answered Hans, casting down his eyes. Then, lifting them again with almost a happy expression, he added, "but it is Hans who can help Mynheer van Holp *this* time."

"How?" asked Peter, making, in his blunt Dutch way, no attempt to conceal his surprise.

"By giving you *this,* mynheer,"—and Hans held forth the missing purse.

"Hurrah!" shouted the boys, taking their cold hands from their pockets to wave them joyfully in the air. But Peter said, "Thank you, Hans Brinker," in a tone that made Hans feel as if the King had knelt to him.

The shout of the delighted boys reached the muffled ears of the fine young gentleman who, under a full pressure of pent-up wrath, was skating toward Amsterdam. A manly boy would have wheeled about at once and hastened to satisfy his curiosity, but Carl only halted and, with his back toward his party, wondered what on earth had happened. There he stood, immovable, until, feeling sure that nothing but the prospect of something to eat could have made them hurrah so heartily, he turned and skated slowly toward his excited comrades.

Meantime Peter had drawn Hans aside from the rest. "How did you know it was my purse?" he asked.

"You paid me three guilders yesterday, mynheer, for making the white-wood chain, telling me that I must buy skates."

"Yes, I remember."

"I saw your purse then; it was of yellow leather."

"And where did you find it today?"

"I left my home this morning, mynheer, in great trouble, and as I skated I took no heed until I stumbled against some lumber, and while I was rubbing my knee I saw your purse nearly hidden under a log."

"That place! Ah, I remember now; just as we were passing it I pulled my muffler from my pocket and probably flirted out the purse at the same time. It would have been gone but for you, Hans. Here"—pouring out the contents—"you—"

"No, mynheer," answered Hans. He spoke quietly, without pretense or any grace of manner, but Peter, somehow, felt rebuked, and put the silver back without a word.

"I like that boy, rich or poor," he thought to himself, then added aloud, "May I ask about this trouble of yours, Hans?"

"Ah, mynheer, it is a sad case—but I have waited here too long. I am going to Leyden to see the great Doctor Boekman—"

"Doctor Boekman!" exclaimed Peter in astonishment.

"Yes, mynheer, and I have not a moment to lose. Goodday!"

"Stay! I am going that way. Come, my lads! Shall we return to Haarlem?"

"Yes," cried the boys eagerly—and off they started.

"Now," said Peter, drawing near Hans, both skimming the

ice so easily and lightly as they skated. on together that they seemed scarce conscious of moving, "we are going to stop at Leyden, and if you are going there only with a message to Doctor Boekman, cannot I do the errand for you? The boys may be too tired to skate so far today, but I will promise to see him early tomorrow if he is to be found in the city."

"Ah, mynheer, that would be serving me indeed; it is not the distance I dread, but leaving my mother so long."

"Is she ill?"

"No, mynheer. It is the father. You may have heard it; how he has been without wit for many a year—ever since the great Schlossen mill was built; but his body has been well and strong. Last night the mother knelt upon the hearth to blow the peat (it is his only delight to sit and watch the live embers, and she will blow them into a blaze every hour of the day to please him). Before she could stir he sprang upon her like a giant and held her close to the fire, all the time laughing and shaking his head. I was on the canal, but I heard the mother scream and ran to her. The father had never loosened his hold and her gown was smoking. I tried to deaden the fire, but with one hand he pushed me off. There was no water in the cottage or I could have done better—and all that time he laughed—such a terrible laugh, mynheer; hardly a sound, but all in his face—I tried to pull her away, but that only made it worse—then—it was dreadful, but could I see the mother burn? I beat him—beat him with a stool. He tossed me away. The gown was on fire! I *would* put it out. I can't remember well after that; I found myself upon the floor and the mother was praying—it seemed to me she was in a blaze, and all the while I could hear that laugh. My sister Gretel screamed out that he was holding the mother close to the very coals, *I* could not tell! Gretel flew to the closet and filled a porringer with the food he liked, and put it upon the floor. Then, mynheer, he left the mother and crawled to it like a little child. She was not burnt, only a part of her clothing—ah, how kind she was to him all night, watching and tending him—he slept in a high fever, with his hands pressed to his head. The mother says he has done that so much of late, as though he felt pain there—Ah, mynheer, I did not mean to tell you. If the father was himself he would not harm even a kitten—"

For a moment the two boys moved on in silence—

"It is terrible," said Peter at last. "How is he today?"

"Very sick, mynheer—"

"Why go for Dr. Boekman, Hans? There are others in Amsterdam who could help him, perhaps;—Boekman is a famous man, sought only by the wealthiest and they often wait upon him in vain."

"He *promised,* mynheer; he promised me yesterday to come to the father in a week—but now that the change has come, we cannot wait—we think the poor father is dying—Oh! mynheer, you can plead with him to come quick—he will not wait a whole week and our father dying—the good meester is so kind—"

"*So kind!*" echoed Peter, in astonishment, "why, he is known as the crossest man in Holland!"

"He looks so because he has no fat and his head is busy, but his heart is kind, I know— Tell the meester what I have told you, mynheer, and he will come."

"I hope so, Hans, with all my heart. You are in haste to turn homeward, I see. Promise me that should you need a friend, you will go to my mother, at Broek. Tell her I bade you see her; and, Hans Brinker—not as a reward—but as a gift—take a few of these guilders."

Hans shook his head resolutely.

"No, no, mynheer—I cannot take it. If I could find work in Broek or at the South mill I would be glad, but it is the same story everywhere—'wait till spring'."

"It is well you speak of it," said Peter eagerly, "for my father needs help at once. Your pretty chain pleased him much—he said, 'that boy has a clean cut, he would be good at carving'— There is to be a carved portal to our new summer-house and father will pay well for the job."

"God is good!" cried Hans in sudden delight, "Oh! mynheer, that would be too much joy—I have never tried big work—but I can do it—I know I can."

"Well, tell my father you are the Hans Brinker of whom I spoke. He will be glad to serve you."

Hans stared in honest surprise.

"Thank you, mynheer."

"Now, Captain," shouted Carl, anxious to appear as good-natured as possible, by way of atonement, "here we are in the midst of Haarlem, and no word from you yet—we await your orders, and we're as hungry as wolves."

Peter made a cheerful answer and turned hurriedly to Hans.

"Come, get something to eat and I will detain you no longer."

What a quick, wistful look Hans threw upon him! Peter wondered that he had not noticed before that the poor boy was hungry.

"Ah, mynheer, even now the mother may need me, the father may be worse—I must not wait. May God care for you"—and, nodding hastily, Hans turned his face homeward and was gone."

"Come, boys," sighed Peter, "now for our lunch!"

XIII

HOMES

IT must not be supposed that our young Dutchmen had already forgotten the great skating race which was to take place on the twentieth. On the contrary, they had thought and spoken of it very often during the day. Even Ben, though he had felt more like a traveler than the rest, had never once, through all the sight-seeing, lost a certain vision of silver skates which, for a week past, had haunted him night and day.

Like a true "John Bull," as Jacob had called him, he never doubted that his English fleetness, English strength, English everything, could at any time enable him, on the ice, to put all Holland to shame, and the rest of the world, too, for that matter. Ben certainly was a superb skater.

Only to the heavy heart of poor Hans had the vision of the silver skates failed to appear during that starry winter night and the brighter sunlit day.

Rychie, Hilda and Katrinka — why, they had scarcely known any other thought than "The race! the race! It will come off on the twentieth!"

These three girls were friends. Though of nearly the same age, talent and station, they were as different as girls could be.

Hilda van Gleck you already know—a warm-hearted, noble girl of fourteen. Rychie van Korbes was beautiful to look upon, far more sparkling and pretty than Hilda, but not half so bright and sunny within. Clouds of pride, of discontent and envy had already gathered in her heart, and were growing bigger and darker every day.

Katrinka was a very lively girl, whose nature was made of a hundred tinkling bells. She was a coquette in her infancy, a coquette in her childhood, and now a coquette in her school-days. Everyone liked her, but who could love her? She was never in earnest. A pleasant face, a pleasant heart, a pleasant manner—these only satisfy for an hour.

How different were the homes of these three girls from the tumbling old cottage where Gretel dwelt. Rychie lived in a beautiful house near Amsterdam, where the carved sideboards were laden with services of silver and gold, and where silken tapestries hung in folds from ceiling to floor.

Hilda's father owned the largest mansion in Broek. Its glittering roof of polished tiles, and its boarded front, painted in half a dozen various colors, were the admiration of the neighborhood.

Katrinka's home, not a mile distant, was the finest of Dutch country-seats. The garden was so stiffly laid out in little paths and patches that the birds might have mistaken it for a great Chinese puzzle with all the pieces spread out ready for use. But in summer it was beautiful.

Carl was both right and wrong when he said that Katrinka and Rychie were furious at the very idea of the peasant, Gretel, joining in the race. He had heard Rychie declare it was "Disgraceful, shameful, *too bad!*" which in Dutch, as in English, is generally the strongest expression an indignant girl can use; and he had seen Katrinka nod her pretty head and heard her sweetly echo, "Shameful, too bad!" as nearly like Rychie as tinkling bells can be like the voice of real anger.

This had satisfied him. He never suspected that had Hilda, not Rychie, first talked with Katrinka upon the subject, the bells would have jingled as willing an echo. She would have said, "Certainly, let her join us," and would have skipped off thinking no more about it. But *now* Katrinka with sweet emphasis pronounced it a shame that a goose-girl, a forlorn little creature like Gretel, should be allowed to spoil the race.

Rychie, being rich and powerful (in a school-girl way), had other followers, besides Katrinka, who were induced to share her opinions because they were either too careless or too cowardly to think for themselves.

Poor little Gretel! Her home was sad and dark enough now Raff Brinker lay moaning upon his rough bed, and his vrouw, forgetting and forgiving everything, bathed his forehead, his lips, weeping and praying that he might not die. Hans, as we know, had started, in desperation, for Leyden to search for Dr. Boekman, and induce him, if possible, to come to their father at once. Gretel, filled with a strange dread, had done the work as well as she could, wiped the rough brick floor, brought peat to build up the slow fire, and melted ice for her mother's use. This accomplished, she seated herself upon a low stool near the bed and begged her mother to try and sleep awhile.

"You are so tired," she whispered, "not once have you closed your eyes since that dreadful hour last night. See, I have straightened the willow bed in the corner and spread everything soft upon it I could find, so that the mother might lie in comfort. Here is your jacket. Take off that pretty dress, I'll fold it away very careful, and put it in the big chest before you go to sleep."

Dame Brinker shook her head without turning her eyes from her husband's face.

"I can watch, mother," urged Gretel, "and I'll wake you every time the father stirs. You are so pale, and your eyes are so red—oh, mother, *do!*"

The child pleaded in vain. Dame Brinker would not leave her post.

Gretel looked at her in troubled silence, wondering whether it were very wicked to care more for one parent than for the other—and sure, yes, quite sure, that she dreaded her father, while she clung to her mother with a love that was almost idolatry.

"Hans loves the father so well," she thought, "why cannot I? Yet I could not help crying when I saw his hand bleed that day, last month, when he snatched the knife—and now, when he moans, how I ache, ache all over. Perhaps I love him, after all, and God will see I am not such a bad, wicked girl as I thought. Yes, I love the poor father—almost as Hans does—not quite, for Hans is stronger and does not fear him. Oh, will that moaning go on forever and ever! Poor mother, how patient she is; *she* never pouts, as I do, about the money that went away so strangely. If he only could, just for one instant, open his eyes and look at us, as Hans does, and tell us where mother's guilders went, I would not care for the rest—yes, I would care—I don't want the poor father to die, to be all blue and cold like Annie Bouman's little sister—I *know* I don't—dear God, I don't want father to die.

"Oh, mother, if Hans were only here he could turn the father some way so the moans would stop—dear! dear! if this sickness lasts, we shall never skate any more. I must send my new skates back to the beautiful lady. Hans and I will not see the race," and Gretel's eyes, that had been dry before, grew full of tears.

"Never cry, child," said her mother soothingly. "This sickness may not be as bad as we think. The father has lain this way before."

Gretel sobbed now.

"Oh, mother, it is not that alone—you do not know all— I am very, very bad and wicked!"

"*You*, Gretel! you, so patient and good!" and a bright, puzzled look beamed for an instant upon the child. "Hush! lovey, you'll wake him."

Gretel hid her face in her mother's lap and tried not to cry.

Her little hand, so thin and brown, lay in the coarse palm of her mother, creased with many a hard day's work. Rychie would have shuddered to touch either, yet they pressed warmly upon each other. Soon Gretel looked up with that dull, homely look which, they say, poor children in shanties are apt to have, and said in a trembling voice:

"The father tried to burn you—he did—I saw him, and he was *laughing!*"

"Hush, child!"

The mother's words came so suddenly and sharply that Raff Brinker, dead as he was to all that was passing round him, twitched slightly upon the bed.

XIV

HAARLEM — THE BOYS HEAR VOICES

REFRESHED and rested, our boys came forth from the coffee-house just as the big clock in the Square, after the manner of certain Holland timekeepers, was striking *two* with its half-hour bell, for half-past *two*.

The captain was absorbed in thought at first, for Hans Brinker's sad story still echoed in his ears. Not until Ludwig rebuked him with a laughing "Wake up, Grandfather!" did he reassume his position as gallant boy-leader of his band.

"Ahem! this way, young gentlemen!"

Haarlem, like Amsterdam, was gayer than usual, in honor of Saint Nicholas.

A strange figure was approaching them. It was a small

man dressed in black, with a short cloak; he wore a wig and a cocked hat from which a long crape streamer was flying.

"Who comes here?" cried Ben, "what a queer-looking object."

"That's the *aanspreeker,*" said Lambert, "someone is dead."

"Is that the way men dress in mourning in this country?"

"Oh, no. The *aanspreeker* attends funerals, and it is his business, when anyone dies, to notify all the friends and relatives."

"What a strange custom."

"Well," said Lambert, "we needn't feel very badly about this particular death, for I see another man has lately been born to the world to fill up the vacant place."

Ben stared. "How do you know that?"

"Don't you see that pretty red pin-cushion hanging on yonder door?" asked Lambert in return.

"Yes."

"Well, that's a boy."

"A boy! What do you mean?"

"I mean that here in Haarlem, whenever a boy is born, the parents have a red pin-cushion put out at the door. If our young friend had been a girl instead of a boy the cushion would have been white. In some places they have much more fanciful affairs, all trimmed with lace, and even among the very poorest houses you will see a bit of ribbon or even a string tied on the door-latch—"

"Look!" almost screamed Ben, "there *is* a white cushion, at the door of that double-jointed house with the funny roof."

"True enough—there's a girl! I tell you what, Captain," called out Lambert, slipping easily into Dutch, "we must get out of this street as soon as possible. It's full of babies! They'll set up a squall in a moment."

The captain laughed. "I shall take you to hear better music than that," he said; "we are just in time to hear the organ of Saint Bavon. The church is open today."

"What! the great Haarlem organ?" asked Ben.

"The same," answered Lambert van Mounen.

Peter was right. The church was open, though not for religious services. Someone was playing upon the organ. As the boys entered a swell of sound rushed forth to meet them. It seemed to bear them, one by one, into the shadows of the building.

Louder and louder it grew until it became like the din and roar of some mighty tempest, or like the ocean surging upon the shore. At last the storm grew silent; hidden birds sprang forth, filling the air with glad, ecstatic music, rising higher and higher until the last faint note was lost in the distance.

To Peter and Ben it seemed that the angels were singing. Their eyes grew dim and their souls dizzy with a strange joy. At last, as if borne upward by invisible hands, they were floating away on the music, all fatigue forgotten, and with no wish but to hear forever those beautiful sounds—when suddenly Van Holp's sleeve was pulled impatiently and a gruff voice beside him asked:

"How long are you going to stay here, Captain—blinking at the ceiling like a sick rabbit? It's high time we started."

"Hush!" whispered Peter, only half aroused.

"Come, man! Let's go," said Carl, giving the sleeve a second pull.

Peter turned reluctantly; he would not detain the boys

against their will. All but Ben were casting rather reproachful glances upon him.

"Well, boys," he whispered, "we will go. Softly now."

"That's the greatest thing I've seen or heard since I've been in Holland!" cried Ben, enthusiastically, as soon as they reached the open air. "It's glorious!"

Lambert, the interpreter, responded with a brisk—

"You may well say so. I believe there are one or two organs nowadays that are said to be as fine, but for years and years this organ of Saint Bavon was the grandest in the world. Handel, the great composer, once chanced to visit Haarlem and of course he hunted up this famous organ. He gained admittance and was playing upon it with all his might, when the regular organist chanced to enter the building. The man stood awe-struck; he was a good player himself, but he had never heard such music before. 'Who is there?' he cried. 'If it is not an angel or the devil, it must be Handel!' When he discovered that it *was* the great musician, he was still more mystified. 'But how is this?' said he; 'you have done impossible things—no ten fingers on earth can play the passages you have given; human hands couldn't control all the keys and stops!' 'I know it,' said Handel, coolly, 'and for that reason I was forced to strike some notes with the end of my nose.' Donder! just think how the old organist must have stared!"

Leaving the church, the boys were soon on the Grand Canal again. As they skated toward Leyden, Lambert said: "I never pass through Haarlem but I think of the story of its little hero."

"Oh, do tell me about him," entreated Ben eagerly.

Lambert was only too willing and related the following

story: "Many years ago, there lived in Haarlem, one of the principal cities of Holland, a sunny-haired boy of gentle disposition. His father was a *sluicer,* that is, a man whose business it was to open and close the sluices, or large oaken gates, that are placed at regular distances across the entrances of the canals, to regulate the amount of water that shall flow into them.

"One lovely autumn afternoon, when the boy was about eight years old, he obtained his parents' consent to carry some cakes to a blind man who lived out in the country, on the other side of the dyke. The little fellow started on his errand with a light heart and, having spent an hour with his grateful friend, he bade him farewell and started on his homeward walk.

"Trudging stoutly along by the canal, he noticed how the autumn rains had swollen the waters. It was growing dark. He was still some distance from home, and in a lonely ravine, when he was startled by the sound of trickling water. Whence did it come? He looked up and saw a small hole in the dyke through which a tiny stream was flowing. Any child in Holland will shudder at the thought of a leak in the dyke! The boy understood the danger at a glance. That little hole, if the water were allowed to trickle through, would soon be a large one, and a terrible inundation would be the result.

"Quick as a flash he saw his duty. He clambered up the heights until he reached the hole. His chubby little finger was thrust in, almost before he knew it. The flowing was stopped! 'Ah!' he thought, with a chuckle of boyish delight, 'the angry waters must stay back now! Haarlem will not be drowned while *I am here!*'

"This was all very well at first, but the night was falling rapidly; chill vapors filled the air. Our little hero began to tremble with cold and dread. He shouted loudly; he screamed,

HIS CHUBBY LITTLE FINGER WAS THRUST IN,
ALMOST BEFORE HE KNEW IT.

'Come here! come here!' but no one came. The cold grew more intense.

"The midnight moon looked down upon that small, solitary form, sitting upon a stone, half-way up the dyke. His head was bent, but he was not asleep, for every now and then one restless hand rubbed feebly the outstretched arm that seemed fastened to the dyke—and often the pale, tearful face turned quickly at some real or fancied sound.

"At daybreak a clergyman, returning from the bedside of a sick parishioner, thought he heard groans as he walked along the top of the dyke. Bending, he saw, far down on the side, a child apparently writhing with pain.

" 'In the name of wonder, child,' he exclaimed, 'what are you doing there?'

" 'I am keeping the water from running out,' was the simple answer of the little hero. 'Tell them to come quick.'

"It is needless to add that they did come quickly and that——"

"The noble little fellow!" interrupted Ben. "Is it a true story?"

"True! Of course it is," said Lambert, kindling. "I have given you the story just as mother told it to me years ago. Why, there is not a child in Holland who does not know it. And, Ben, you may not think so, but that little boy represents the spirit of the whole country. Not a leak can show itself anywhere either in its politics, honor or public safety, but that a million fingers are ready to stop it at any cost."

"Whew!" cried Master Ben, "big talking that!"

"It's *true* talk anyway," rejoined Lambert, so very quietly that Ben wisely resolved to make no further comment.

XV

ON THE CANAL

THE skating season had commenced unusually early; our boys were by no means alone upon the ice. The afternoon was so fine that men, women and children, bent upon enjoying the holiday, had flocked to the grand canal from far and near. Saint Nicholas had evidently remembered the favorite pastime; shining new skates were everywhere to be seen. Whole families were skimming their way to Haarlem or Leyden or the neighboring villages.

Boys and girls were chasing each other and hiding behind the one-horse sleds, that, loaded high with peat or timber, pursued their cautious way along the track marked out as "safe."

Suddenly a beautiful ice-boat with reefed sail and flying

streamers swept leisurely by. Its deck was filled with children muffled up to their chins. They were singing a chorus in honor of Saint Nicholas. The music, starting in the discord of a hundred childish voices, floated, as it rose, into exquisite harmony:

> "Friend of sailors, and of children!
> Double claim have we,
> As in youthful joy we're sailing,
> O'er a frozen sea!
> > Nicholas! Saint Nicholas!
> > Let us sing to thee.
>
> "While through wintry air we're rushing,
> As our voices blend,
> Are you near us? Do you hear us,
> Nicholas, our friend?
> > Nicholas! Saint Nicholas!
> > Love can never end.
>
> "Sunny sparkles, bright before us,
> Chase away the cold!
> Hearts where sunny thoughts are welcome,
> Never can grow old—
> > Nicholas! Saint Nicholas!—
> > Never can grow old!
>
> "Pretty gift and loving lesson,
> Festival and glee,
> Bid us thank thee as we're sailing
> O'er the frozen sea—
> > Nicholas! Saint Nicholas!
> > So we sing to thee!"

The last note died away in the distance. Our boys, who in their vain efforts to keep up with the boat, had felt that they were skating backward, turned to look at one another.

"How beautiful that was!" exclaimed Van Mounen.

"Just like a dream!" said Ludwig

Jacob drew close to Ben, giving his usual approving nod, as he spoke:

"Dat ish goot. Dat ish te pest vay—*I* shay petter to take to Leyden mit a poat!"

"Take a boat!" exclaimed Ben in dismay—"why, man, our plan was to *skate,* not to be carried like little children——"

The boys laughed, but exchanged uneasy glances. It would be great fun to jump on an ice-boat, if they had a chance; but to abandon so shamefully their grand undertaking—who could think of such a thing?

An animated discussion arose at once.

Captain Peter brought his party to a halt.

"Boys," said he, "it strikes me that we should consult Jacob's wishes in this matter. He started the excursion, you know."

"Pooh!" sneered Carl, throwing a contemptuous glance at Jacob, "who's tired? We can rest all night at Leyden."

Ludwig and Lambert looked anxious and disappointed. It was no slight thing to lose the credit of having skated all the way from Broek to The Hague and back again, but both agreed that Jacob should decide the question.

Good-natured, tired Jacob! He read the popular sentiment at a glance.

"Oh! no," he said, in Dutch. "I was joking. We will skate, of course."

The boys gave a delighted shout and started on again with renewed vigor—

All but Jacob. He tried his best not to seem fatigued and, by not saying a word, saved his breath and energy for the great business of skating. But in vain. Before long the stout body grew heavier and heavier—the tottering limbs weaker and weaker, and he fell heavily upon the ice.

"Hello!" cried Van Mounen. "There goes Poot!"

Ben sprang hastily forward.

"Jacob! Jacob, are you hurt?"

Peter and Carl were lifting him. His face was white. It seemed like a dead face—even the good-natured look was gone.

A crowd collected. Peter unbuttoned the poor boy's jacket, loosened his red muffler, and blew between the parted lips.

"Stand off, good people!" he cried, "give him air!"

"Lay him down," called out a woman from the crowd.

"Stand him upon his feet," shouted another.

"Give him wine," growled a stout fellow who was driving a loaded sled

"Yes! yes, give him wine!" echoed everybody.

Ludwig and Lambert shouted in concert:

"Wine! wine! Who has wine?"

A sleepy-eyed Dutchman began to fumble mysteriously under the heaviest of blue jackets, saying as he did so:

"Not so much noise, young masters, not so much noise! The boy was a fool to faint off like a girl."

"Wine, quick!" cried Peter, who, with Ben's help, was rubbing Jacob from head to foot.

Ludwig stretched forth his hand imploringly toward the Dutchman, who, with an air of great importance, was still fumbling beneath the jacket.

"*Do* hurry! He will die! Has anyone else any wine?"

"He *is* dead!" said an awful voice from among the bystanders.

This startled the Dutchman.

"Have a care!" he said, reluctantly drawing forth a small blue flask, "this is schnaps. A little is enough."

A little *was* enough. The paleness gave way to a faint flush. Jacob opened his eyes and — half bewildered, half

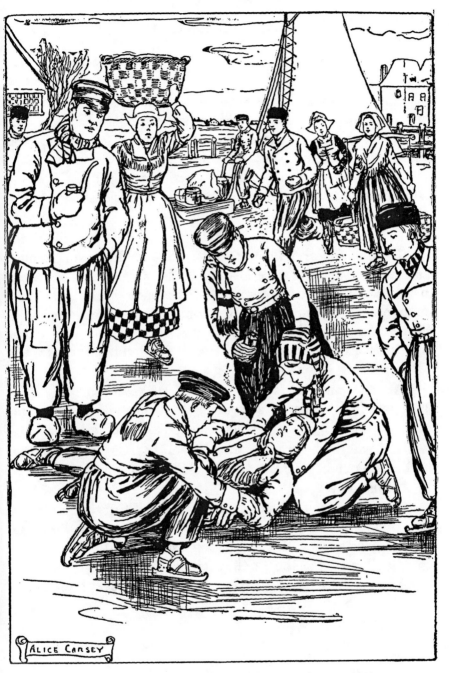

"YES, YES, GIVE HIM WINE!" ECHOED EVERYBODY.

ashamed — feebly tried to free himself from those who were supporting him.

There was no alternative now for the party, but to have their exhausted comrade carried, in some way, to Leyden. As for expecting him to skate any more that day, the thing was impossible. In truth, by this time each boy began to entertain secret yearnings towards ice-boats, and to avow a Spartan resolve not to desert Jacob. Fortunately a gentle, steady breeze was setting southward.

Peter hailed the first sail that appeared; the men in the stern would not even look at him. Three drays on runners came along but they were already loaded to the utmost. Then an ice-boat, a beautiful, tempting little one, whizzed past like an arrow. The boys had just time to stare eagerly at it when it was gone. In despair, they resolved to prop up Jacob with their strong arms, as well as they could, and take him to the nearest village.

At that moment a very shabby ice-boat came in sight. With but little hope of success, Peter hailed it, at the same time taking off his hat and flourishing it in the air.

The sail was lowered, then came the scraping sound of the brake, and a pleasant voice called out from the deck:

"What now?"

"Will you take us on?" cried Peter, hurrying with his companions as fast as he could, for the boat was "bringing to" some distance ahead, "will you take us on?"

"We'll pay for the ride!" shouted Carl.

The man on board scarcely noticed him except to mutter something about it not being a canal-boat. Still looking toward Peter he asked:

"How many?"

"Six."

"Well, it's Nicholas' day—up with you! Young gentleman sick?" (nodding towards Jacob).

"Yes—broken down—skated all the way from Broek," answered Peter. "Do you go to Leyden?"

"That's as the wind says—it's blowing that way now. Scramble up!"

Poor Jacob! It was as much as the boys could do to hoist him into the boat. All were in at last. The owner of the boat, puffing away at his pipe, let out the sail, lifted the brake, and sat in the stern with folded arms.

"Whew! How fast we go!" cried Ben, "this is something like! Feel better, Jacob?"

"Much petter, I tanks you."

"Oh, you'll be as good as new in ten minutes. This makes a fellow feel like a bird."

Jacob nodded and blinked his eyes.

"Don't go to sleep, Jacob; it's too cold. You might never wake up, you know. Persons often freeze to death in that way."

"I no sleep," said Jacob confidently—and in two minutes he was snoring.

Carl and Ludwig laughed.

"We must wake him!" cried Ben, "it is dangerous, I tell you—Jacob! Ja-a-c——"

Captain Peter interfered, for three of the boys were helping Ben for the fun of the thing.

"Nonsense! don't shake him! Let him alone, boys. One never snores like that when one's freezing. Cover him up with something. Here, this cloak will do."

"There," said Peter, tenderly adjusting the garment, "let him sleep. He will be frisky as a lamb when he wakes."

It was a grand sail, or ride, I scarce know which to call it; perhaps "fly" would be the best word; for the boys felt very much as Sinbad did when, tied to the roc's leg, he darted through the clouds; or as Bellerophon felt when he shot through the air on the back of his winged horse Pegasus. Sailing, riding or flying, whichever it was, everything was rushing past, backward—and, before they had time to draw a long breath, Leyden itself, with its high, peaked roofs flew half-way to meet them.

When the city came in sight it was high time to waken the sleeper. That feat accomplished, Peter's prophecy came to pass. Master Jacob was quite restored and in excellent spirits.

The boat owner made a feeble remonstrance when Peter, with hearty thanks, endeavored to slip some silver pieces into his tough, brown palm.

"Ye see, young master," said he, drawing away his hand, "the regular line o' trade's *one* thing, and a favor's another."

"I know it," said Peter, "but those boys and girls of yours will want sweets when you get home. Buy them some in the name of Saint Nicholas."

The man grinned. "Aye, true enough; I've young 'uns in plenty—a clean boat-load of them. You are a sharp young master at guessing."

This time, the knotty hand hitched forward again, quite carelessly, it seemed, but its palm was upward. Peter hastily dropped in the money and moved away.

The sail soon came tumbling down. Scrape, scrape went the brake, scattering an ice shower round the boat.

"Good-bye!" shouted the boys, seizing their skates and leaping from the deck one by one, "many thanks to you!"

"Ho! for an inn!" cried Peter, as they stepped into the city. "Be brisk, my fine fellows!"

XVI

THE boys soon found an unpretending establishment near Broad Street, with a funnily painted lion over the door. This was the Red Lion, kept by Huygens Kleef, a stout Dutchman with short legs and a very long pipe.

By this time they were in a ravenous condition. The lunch taken at Haarlem had served only to give them an appetite, and this had been heightened by their exercise and swift sail upon the canal.

"Come, mine host! give us what you can!" cried Peter, rather pompously.

"I can give you anything—everything," answered Mynheer Kleef, performing a bow with difficulty.

"Well, give us sausage and pudding."

"Ah, mynheer, the sausage is all gone. There is no pudding."

"Salmagundi, then, and plenty of it."

"That is out also, young master."

"Eggs, and be quick."

"Winter eggs are *very* poor eating," answered the innkeeper, puckering his lips and lifting his eyebrows.

"No eggs?—well—caviare."

The Dutchman raised his fat hands—

"Caviare! That is made of gold! Who has caviare to sell?"

Peter had sometimes eaten it at home; he knew that it

95

was made of the roes of the sturgeon and certain other large fish, but he had no idea of its cost.

"Well, mine host, what have you?"

"What have I? Everything. I have rye bread, sour-krout, potato salad, and the fattest herring in Leyden."

"What do you say, boys?" asked the captain, "will that do?"

"Yes," cried the famished youths, "if he'll only be quick."

Mynheer moved off like one walking in his sleep, but soon opened his eyes wide at the miraculous manner in which his herring were made to disappear. Next came, or rather went, potato salad, rye bread and coffee—then Utrecht water flavored with orange, and, finally, slices of dry gingerbread This last delicacy was not on the regular bill of fare, but Mynheer Kleef, driven to extremes, solemnly produced it from his own private stores, and gave only a placid blink when his voracious young travelers started up, declaring they had eaten enough.

Softly rubbing his hands, he asked:

"Will your worships have beds?"

"Will your worships have beds?" mocked Carl—"what do you mean? Do we look sleepy?"

"Not at all, master; but I would cause them to be warmed and aired. None sleep under damp sheets at the Red Lion."

"Ah, I understand. Shall we come back here to sleep, Captain?"

Peter was accustomed to finer lodgings, but this was a frolic.

"Why not?" he replied, "we can fare excellently here."

"Your worship speaks only the truth," said mynheer with great deference.

"How fine to be called 'your worship'," laughed Ludwig aside to Lambert, while Peter replied:

"Well, mine host, you may get the rooms ready by nine."

"I have one beautiful chamber, with three beds, that will hold all your worships," said Mynheer Kleef coaxingly.

"That will do."

"Whew!" whistled Carl when they reached the street.

Ludwig started. "What now?"

"Nothing—only Mynheer Kleef of the Red Lion little thinks how we shall make things spin in that same room tonight—we'll set the bolsters flying!"

"Order!" cried the captain. "Now, boys, I must seek this great Doctor Boekman before I sleep. If he is in Leyden it will be no great task to find him, for he always puts up at the Golden Eagle when he comes here. I wonder that you did not all go to bed at once—still, as you are awake, what say you to walking with Ben up by the Museum or the Stadhuis?"

"Agreed," said Ludwig and Lambert; but Jacob preferred to go with Peter. In vain Ben tried to persuade him to remain at the inn and rest. He declared that he never felt "petter," and wished of all things to take a look at the city, for it was his first "stop mit Leyden."

"Oh, it will not harm him," said Lambert. "How long the day has been—and what glorious sport we have had. It hardly seems possible that we left Broek only this morning."

Jacob yawned.

"I have enjoyed it well," he said, "but it seems to me at least a week since we started."

Carl laughed and muttered something about "twenty naps——"

"Here we are at the corner; remember, we all meet at the Red Lion at eight," said the captain, as he and Jacob walked away.

XVII

THE RED LION BECOMES DANGEROUS

THE boys were glad to find a blazing fire awaiting them upon their return to the Red Lion. Carl and his party were there first. Soon afterward Peter and Jacob came in. They had inquired in vain concerning Dr. Boekman. All they could ascertain was that he had been seen in Haarlem that morning.

'As for his being in Leyden," the landlord of the Golden Eagle had said to Peter, "the thing is impossible. He always lodges here when in town. By this time there would be a crowd at my door waiting to consult him—Bah! people make such fools of themselves!"

"He is called a great surgeon," said Peter.

"Yes, the greatest in Holland. But what of that? What of being the greatest pill-choker and knife-slasher in the world? The man is a bear. Only last month, on this very spot, he called me *a pig*, before three customers!"

"No!" exclaimed Peter, trying to look surprised and indignant.

"Yes, master—A PIG," repeated the landlord, puffing at his pipe with an injured air. "Bah! if he did not pay fine prices and bring customers to my house I would sooner see him in the Vliet Canal than give him lodgment."

Perhaps mine host felt that he was speaking too openly

to a stranger, or it may be he saw a smile lurking in Peter's
face, for he added sharply:

"Come, now, what more do you wish? Supper? Beds?"

"No, mynheer; I am but searching for Dr. Boekman."

"Go find him. He is not in Leyden."

Peter was not to be put off so easily. After receiving
a few more rough words, he succeeded in obtaining permission to leave a note for the famous surgeon, or rather, he
bought from his amiable landlord the. privilege of writing
it there, and a promise that it should be promptly delivered
when Doctor Boekman arrived. This accomplished, Peter
and Jacob returned to the Red Lion.

This inn had once been a fine house, the home of a rich
burgher, but, having grown old and shabby, it had passed
through many hands until finally it had fallen into the possession of Mynheer Kleef. The public room on the ground
floor was the landlord's joy and pride. If you will but open
your mind's eye, you may look into the apartment.

Imagine a large, bare room, with a floor that seemed to
be made of squares cut out of glazed earthen pie-dishes, first
a yellow piece, then a red, until the whole looked like a vast
checker-board. Fancy a dozen high-backed wooden chairs
standing around; then a great hollow chimney-place all aglow
with its blazing fire, reflected a hundred times in the polished
steel firedogs; a tiled hearth, tiled sides, tiled top, with a
Dutch sentence upon it; and over all, high above one's head,
a narrow mantel-shelf, filled with shining brass candlesticks,
pipe-lighters and tinder-boxes. Then see, in one end of the
room, three pine tables; in the other, a closet and a deal
dresser. The latter is filled with mugs, dishes, pipes, tankards,
earthen and glass bottles, and is guarded at one end by a
brass-hooped keg standing upon long legs. Everything dim

with tobacco smoke, but otherwise clean as soap and sand can make it. Next, picture two sleepy, shabby-looking men, in wooden shoes, seated near the glowing fireplace, hugging their knees and smoking short, stumpy pipes; Mynheer Kleef walking softly and heavily about, clad in leather knee breeches, felt shoes and a green jacket wider than it is long:—then throw a heap of skates in the corner and put six tired, well-dressed boys, in various attitudes, upon the wooden chairs, and you will see the coffee-room of the Red Lion just as it appeared at nine o'clock on the evening of December 6th, 184–. For supper, gingerbread again; slices of Dutch sausage; rye bread sprinkled with anise-seed; pickles; a bottle of Utrecht water, and a pot of very mysterious coffee. The boys were ravenous enough to take all they could get, and pronounce it excellent. Ben made wry faces, but Jacob declared he had never eaten a better meal. After they had laughed and talked awhile, and counted their money by way of settling a discussion that arose concerning their expenses, the captain marched his company off to bed, led on by a greasy pioneer-boy who carried skates and a candlestick instead of an axe.

One of the ill-favored men by the fire had shuffled towards the dresser and was ordering a mug of beer, just as Ludwig, who brought up the rear, was stepping from the apartment.

"I don't like that fellow's eye," he whispered to Carl, "he looks like a pirate, or something of that kind."

"Looks like a granny!" answered Carl in sleepy disdain.

Ludwig laughed uneasily.

"Granny or no granny," he whsipered, "I tell you he looks just like one of those men in the 'voetspoelen'."

"Pooh!" sneered Carl, "I knew it. That picture was too much for you. Look sharp now, and see if yon fellow with the candle doesn't look like the other villain."

"No, indeed, his face is as honest as a Gouda cheese. But I say, Carl, that really was a horrid picture."

"Humph! Why did you stare at it so long?"

"I couldn't help it."

By this time the boys had reached the "beautiful room with three beds in it." A dumpy little maiden with long earrings met them at the doorway, dropped them a courtesy, and passed out. She carried a long-handled thing that resembled a frying-pan with a cover.

"I am glad to see that," said Van Mounen to Ben.

"What?"

"Why, the warming-pan! It's full of hot ashes; she's been heating our beds."

"Oh! a warming-pan, eh! Much obliged to her, I'm sure," said Ben, too sleepy to make any further comment.

Meantime, Ludwig still talked of the picture that had made such a strong impression upon him. He had seen it in a shop window during their walk. It was a poorly painted thing, representing two men tied back to back, standing on shipboard, surrounded by a group of seamen who were preparing to cast them together into the sea. This mode of putting prisoners to death was called *voetspoelen,* or feet-washing, and was practiced by the Dutch upon the pirates of Dunkirk in 1605, and again by the Spaniards upon the Dutch in the horrible massacre that followed the siege of Haarlem. Bad as the painting was, the expression upon the pirates' faces was well given. Sullen and despairing as they seemed, they wore such a cruel, malignant aspect that Ludwig had felt a secret satisfaction in contemplating their helpless condition. He might have forgotten the scene by this time but for that ill-looking man by the fire. Now, while he capered about, boy-like, and threw himself with an antic into his bed, he inwardly hoped that the 'voetspoelen' would not haunt his dreams.

It was a cold, cheerless room; a fire had been newly kindled in the burnished stove and seemed to shiver even while trying to burn. The windows, with their funny little panes, were bare and shiny, and the cold, waxed floor looked like a sheet of yellow ice. Three rush-bottomed chairs stood stiffly against the wall, alternating with three narrow wooden bed-steads that made the room look like the deserted ward of a hospital. At any other time the boys would have found it quite impossible to sleep in pairs, especially in such narrow quarters; but tonight they lost all fear of being crowded and longed only to lay their weary bodies upon the feather beds that lay lightly upon each cot. Had the boys been in Germany instead of Holland they might have been covered, also, by a bed of down or feathers. This peculiar form of luxury was at that time adopted only by wealthy or eccentric Hollanders.

Ludwig, as we have seen, had not quite lost his friskiness, but the other boys, after one or two feeble attempts at pillow-firing, composed themselves for the night with the greatest dignity. Nothing like fatigue for making boys behave themselves.

"Good-night, boys!" said Peter's voice from under the covers."

"Good-night," called back everybody but Jacob, who already lay snoring beside the captain.

"I say," shouted Carl, after a moment, "don't sneeze, anybody. Ludwig's in a fright!"

"No such thing," retorted Ludwig in a smothered voice. Then there was a little whispered dispute, which was ended by Carl saying:

"For *my* part, I don't know what fear is. But you really are a timid fellow, Ludwig."

Ludwig grunted sleepily, but made no further reply.

———————

It was the middle of the night. The fire had shivered itself to death and in place of its gleams little squares of moonlight lay upon the floor, slowly, slowly shifting their way across the room. Something else was moving also, but they did not see it. Sleeping boys keep but a poor lookout. During the early hours of the night, Jacob Poot had been gradually but surely winding himself with all the bed covers. He now lay like a monster chrysalis beside the half frozen Peter, who accordingly was skating with all his might over the coldest, bleakest of dreamland icebergs.

Something else, I say, besides the moonlight, was moving across the bare, polished floor—moving not quite so slowly, but quite as stealthily.

Wake up, Ludwig! The voetspoelen pirate is growing real!

No. Ludwig does not waken, but he moans in his sleep.

Does not Carl hear it—Carl the brave, the fearless!

No. Carl is dreaming of the race.

And Jacob? Van Mounen? Ben?

Not they. They, too, are dreaming of the race; and Katrinka is singing through their dreams—laughing, flitting past them. Now and then a wave from the great organ surges through their midst.

Still the thing moves, slowly, slowly.

Peter! Captain Peter, there is danger!

Peter heard no call; but, in his dream, he slid a few thousand feet from one iceberg to another, and the shock awoke him.

Whew! How cold he was! He gave a hopeless, desperate tug at the chrysalis. In vain; sheet, blanket and spread were firmly wound about Jacob's inanimate form. Peter looked drowsily toward the window.

"Clear moonlight," he thought, "we shall have pleasant weather tomorrow. Hello! what's that?"

He saw the moving thing, or rather something black crouching upon the floor, for it had halted as Peter stirred.

He watched in silence.

Soon it moved again, nearer and nearer. It was a man crawling upon hands and feet!

The captain's first impulse was to call out, but he took an instant to consider matters.

The creeper had a shining knife in one hand. This was ugly, but Peter was naturally self-possessed. When the head turned, Peter's eyes were closed as if in sleep, but at other times nothing could be keener, sharper than the captain's gaze.

Closer, closer crept the robber. His back was very near Peter now. The knife was laid softly upon the floor; one careful arm reached forth stealthily to drag the clothes from the chair by the captain's bed—the robbery was commenced.

Now was Peter's time! Holding his breath, he sprang up and leaped with all his strength upon the robber's back, stunning the rascal with the force of the blow. The robber began to struggle, but Peter sat like a giant astride the prostrate form.

"If you stir," said the brave boy in as terrible a voice as he could command, "stir but one inch, I will plunge this knife into your neck. Boys! Boys! wake up!" he shouted, still pressing down the black head and holding the knife at pricking distance, "Give us a hand! I've got him! I've got him!"

The chrysalis rolled over, but made no other sign.

"Up, boys!" cried Peter, never budging. "Ludwig! Lambert! Thunder! Are you all dead?"

Dead! not they. Van Mounen and Ben were on their feet in an instant.

"Hey! What now?" they shouted.

"I've got a robber here," said Peter, coolly. "(Lie still, you scoundrel, or I'll slice your head off!) Now, boys, cut out your bed-cord—plenty of time—he's a dead man if he stirs."

Peter felt that he weighed a thousand pounds. So he did, with that knife in his hand. The man growled and swore, but dared not move.

Ludwig was up by this time. He had a great jack-knife, the pride of his heart, in his breeches' pocket. It could do good service now. They bared the bedstead in a moment. It was laced backward and forward with a rope.

"I'll cut it," cried Ludwig, sawing away at the knot, "hold him tight, Peter!"

"Never fear!" answered the captain, giving the robber a warning prick.

The boys were soon pulling at the rope like good fellows. It was out at last—a long, stout piece.

"Now, boys," commanded the captain, "lift up his rascally arms! Cross his hands over his back! That's right—excuse me for being in the way—tie them tight!"

"Yes, and his feet, too, the villain!" cried the boys in great excitement, tying knot after knot with Herculean jerks.

The prisoner changed his tone.

"Oh—oh!" he moaned, "spare a poor sick man—I was but walking in my sleep."

"Ugh!" grunted Lambert, still tugging away at the rope, "asleep, were you? Well, we'll wake you up."

The man uttered fierce oaths between his teeth—then cried in a piteous voice, "Unbind me, good young masters! I have five little children at home. By Saint Bavon I swear to give you each a ten-guilder piece if you will but free me!"

"Ha! ha!" laughed Peter.

"Ha! ha!" laughed the other boys.

Then came threats—threats that made Ludwig fairly shudder, though he continued to bind and tie with redoubled energy.

"Hold up! Mynheer housebreaker," said Van Mounen in a warning voice. "That knife is very near your throat. If you make the captain nervous there is no telling what may happen."

The robber took the hint and fell into a sullen silence.

Just at this moment the chrysalis upon the bed stirred and sat erect.

"What's the matter?" he asked, without opening his eyes.

"Matter!" echoed Ludwig, half trembling, half laughing, "Get up, Jacob. Here's work for you. Come, sit on this fellow's back while we get into our clothes; we're half perished."

"What fellow? Donder!"

"Hurrah for Poot!" cried all the boys, as Jacob, sliding quickly to the floor, bedclothes and all, took in the state of affairs at a glance and sat heavily beside Peter on the robber's back.

Oh, didn't the fellow groan then!

"No use in holding him down any longer, boys," said Peter, rising, but bending as he did so to draw a pistol from his man's belt. "You see I've been keeping guard over this pretty little weapon for the last ten minutes. It's cocked and the least wriggle might have set it off. No danger now.

I must dress myself. You and I, Lambert, will go for the police. I'd no idea it was so cold."

"Where is Carl?" asked one of the boys.

They looked at one another. Carl certainly was not among them.

"Oh!" cried Ludwig, frightened at last, "where is he? Perhaps he's had a fight with the robber and got killed."

"Not a bit of it," said Peter quietly, as he buttoned his stout jacket. "Look under the beds."

They did so. Carl was not there

Just then they heard a commotion on the stairway. Ben hastened to open the door. The landlord almost tumbled in; he was armed with a big blunderbuss. Two or three lodgers followed; then the daughter, with an upraised frying-pan in one hand and a candle in the other; and, behind her, looking pale and frightened, the gallant Carl!

"There's your man, mine host," said Peter, nodding toward the prisoner.

Mine host raised his blunderbuss, the girl screamed, and Jacob, more nimble than usual, rolled quickly from the robber's back.

"Don't fire," cried Peter, "he is tied, hand and foot. Let's roll him over and see what he looks like."

Carl stepped briskly forward, with a blustering "Yes. *We'll* turn him over in a way he won't like. Lucky we've caught him!"

"Ha! ha!" laughed Ludwig, "where were you, Master Carl?"

"Where was I?" retorted Carl, angrily, "why, I went to give the alarm, to be sure!"

All the boys exchanged glances, but they were too happy and elated to say anything ill-natured. Carl certainly was bold enougn now. He took the lead while three others aided him in turning the helpless man.

While the robber lay, face up, scowling and muttering, Ludwig took the candlestick from the girl's hand.

"I must have a good look at the beauty," he said, drawing closer, but the words were no sooner spoken than he turned pale and started so violently that he almost dropped the candle.

"*The voetspoelen!*" he cried. "Why, boys, it's the man who sat by the fire!"

"Of course it is," answered Peter. "We counted our money before him, like simpletons. But what have we to do with voetspoelen, Brother Ludwig? A month in jail is punishment enough."

The landlord's daughter had left the room. She now ran in, holding up a pair of huge wooden shoes. "See, father," she cried, "here are his great ugly boots. It's the man that we put in the next room after the young masters went to bed. Ah! it was wrong to send the poor young gentlemen up here so far out of sight and sound."

"The scoundrel!" hissed the landlord, "he has disgraced my house. I will go for the police at once!"

In less than fifteen minutes two drowsy looking officers were in the room. After telling Mynheer Kleef that he must appear early in the morning with the boys and make his complaint before a magistrate, they marched off with their prisoner.

One would think the captain and his band could have slept no more that night, but the mooring has not yet been found that can prevent youth and an easy conscience from drifting down the river of dreams. The boys were too much fatigued to let so slight a thing as capturing a robber bind them to wakefulness. They were soon in bed again, floating away to strange scenes made of familiar things.

XVIII

BEFORE THE COURT

YOU may believe the landlord's daughter bestirred herself to prepare a good meal for the boys next morning. Mynheer had a Chinese gong that could make more noise than a dozen breakfast bells. Its hideous alarm, clanging through the house generally startled the drowsiest lodgers into activity, but the maiden would not allow it to be sounded this morning.

"Let the brave young gentlemen sleep," she said to the greasy kitchen boy, "they shall be warmly fed when they awaken."

It was ten o'clock when Captain Peter and his band came straggling down one by one.

"A pretty hour," said mine host, gruffly. "It is high time we were before the court. Fine business this for a respectable inn. You will testify truly, young masters, that you found most excellent fare and lodgment at the Red Lion?"

"Of course we will," answered Carl, saucily, "and pleasant company, too, though they visit at rather unseasonable hours."

A stare and a "humph!" was all the answer mynheer made to this, but the daughter was more communicative. Shaking her ear-rings at Carl, she said sharply:

"Not so very pleasant, either, master traveler, if one could judge by the way *you* ran away from it!"

"Impertinent creature!" hissed Carl under his breath, as he began busily to examine his skate-straps. Meantime the kitchen boy, listening outside at the crack of the door, doubled himself with silent laughter.

After breakfast the boys went to the police court, accompanied by Huygens Kleef and his daughter. Mynheer's testimony was principally to the effect that such a thing as a robbery at the Red Lion had been unheard of until last night; and as for the Red Lion, it was a most respectable inn, as respectable as any house in Leyden. Each boy, in turn, told all he knew of the affair, and identified the prisoner in the box as the same man who entered their room in the dead of night. Ludwig was surprised to find that the robber was a man of ordinary size—especially after he had described him, under oath, to the court as a tremendous fellow, with great square shoulders, and legs of prodigious weight. Jacob swore that he was awakened by the robber kicking and thrashing upon the floor; and, immediately afterward, Peter and the rest (feeling sorry that they had not explained the matter to their sleepy comrade) testified that the man had not moved a muscle from the moment the point of the dagger touched his throat, until, bound from head to foot, he was rolled over for inspection. The landlord's daughter made one boy blush, and all the court smile, by declaring that, "if it hadn't been for that handsome young gentleman there" (pointing to Peter) they "might have all been murdered in their beds; for the dreadful man had a great, shining knife most as long as your honor's arm," and *she* believed "the handsome young gentleman had struggled hard enough to get it away from him, but he was too modest, bless him! to say so."

Finally, after a little questioning and cross-questioning from the public prosecutor the witnesses were dismissed and the robber was handed over to the consideration of the criminal court.

"The scoundrel!" said Carl savagely, when the boys reached the street. "He ought to be sent to jail at once. If I had been in your place, Peter, I certainly should have killed him outright!"

"He was fortunate, then, in falling into gentler hands," was Peter's quiet reply. "It appears he has been arrested before under a charge of housebreaking. He did not succeed in robbing this time, but he broke the door-fastenings, and that, I believe, makes a burglary in the eye of the law. He was armed with a knife, too, and that makes it worse for him, poor fellow!"

"Poor fellow!" mimicked Carl, "one would think he was your brother!"

"So he is my brother, and yours, too, Carl Schummel, for that matter," answered Peter, looking into Carl's eye. "We cannot say what we might have become under other circumstances. *We* have been bolstered up from evil, since the hour we were born. A happy home and good parents might have made that man a fine fellow instead of what he is. God grant that the law may cure and not crush him!"

"Amen to that!" said Lambert heartily, while Ludwig van Holp looked at his brother in such a bright, proud way that Jacob Poot, who was an only son, wished from his heart that the little form buried in the old church at home had lived to grow up beside him.

"Humph!" said Carl. "It's very well to be saintly and forgiving, and all that sort of thing, but I'm naturally hard. All these fine ideas seem to rattle off of me like hailstones— and it's nobody's business, either, if they do."

Peter recognized a touch of good feeling in this clumsy confession; holding out his hand, he said in a frank, hearty tone:

"Come, lad, shake hands and let us be good friends even if we don't exactly agree on all questions."

"We do agree better than you think," sulked Carl, as he returned Peter's grasp.

"All right," responded Peter briskly. "Now, Van Mounen, we await Benjamin's wishes. Where would he like to go?"

"To the Egyptian Museum," answered Lambert, after holding a brief consultation with Ben.

"That is on Broad Street. To the Museum let it be. Come, boys!"

XIX

LEYDEN

THE boys arrived at the Museum and were soon examining its extensive collection of curiosities, receiving a new insight into Egyptian life, ancient and modern. Ben and Lambert had often visited the British Museum, but that did not prevent them from being surprised at the richness of the Leyden collection. There were household utensils, wearing apparel, weapons, musical instruments, sarcophagi, and mummies of men, women, and cats, ibexes and other creatures. They saw a massive gold armlet that had been worn by an Egyptian king at a time when some of these same mummies, perhaps, were nimbly treading the streets of Thebes; and jewels and trinkets such as Pharaoh's daughter wore, and the children of Israel borrowed when they departed out of Egypt.

There were other interesting relics, from Rome and Greece, and some curious Roman pottery which had been discovered in digging near The Hague—relics of the days when the countrymen of Julius Cæsar had settled there.

When the boys left this Museum they went to another and saw a wonderful collection of fossil animals, skeletons, birds, minerals, precious stones and other natural specimens, but as they were not learned men they could only walk about and stare, enjoy the little knowledge of natural history they possessed, and wish with all their hearts they had acquired more.

They also obtained admittance to a tea-garden, which in summer was a favorite resort of the citizens, and, passing naked oaks and fruit-trees, ascended a high mound which stood in the center. This was the site of a round tower now in ruins.

As the boys walked about on the top of its stone wall they could get but a poor view of the surrounding city.

Poot was bending over the edge of the high wall. "It would be just like him to grow dizzy and tumble off," thought Ben, as he turned impatiently away. "If the fellow, with his weak head, knew no better than to be venturesome, why let him tumble. Horror! what meant that heavy, crashing sound?"

Ben could not stir. He could only gasp:

"Jacob!"

"Jacob!" cried another startled voice, and another. Ready to faint, Ben managed to turn his head. He saw a crowd of boys on the edge of the wall opposite, but Jacob was not there!

"Good Heaven!" he cried, springing forward, "where is my cousin?"

The crowd parted. It was only four boys, after all. There sat Jacob in their midst, holding his sides and laughing heartily.

"Did I frighten you all?" he said in his native Dutch. "Well, I will tell you how it was. There was a big stone lying on the wall and I put my—my foot out just to push it a little, you see—and the first thing I knew, down went the stone all the way to the bottom and left me sitting here on top with both feet in the air. If I had not thrown myself back at that moment, I certainly would have rolled over after the stone. Well, it is no matter. Help me up, boys."

"You are hurt, Jacob!" said Ben, seeing a shade of seriousness pass over his cousin's face as they lifted him to his feet.

Jacob tried to laugh again. "Oh, no—I feels little hurt ven I stant up, but it ish no matter."

The monument to Van der Werf in the Hooglandsche Kerk was not accessible that day, but the boys spent a few pleasant moments in the Stadhuis or Town Hall, a long, irregular structure, somewhat in the Gothic style, uncouth in architecture, but picturesque from age. Its little steeple, tuneful with bells, seemed to have been borrowed from some other building and hastily clapped on as a finishing touch.

The Town Hall, as well as the Egyptian Museum, is on Broad Street, the longest and finest street in Leyden. It has no canal running through it, and the houses, painted in every variety of color, have a picturesque effect as they stand with their gable ends to the street.

Ben, as he scanned the buildings on the Rapenburg Canal, was somewhat disappointed in the appearance of the great University of Leyden. But when he remembered the great men in religion, learning and science who had once studied there, he was quite willing to forego architectural beauty.

Peter and Jacob regarded the building with even a deeper, more practical interest, for they were to enter it as students, in the course of a few months.

"Poor Don Quixote would have run a hopeless tilt in this part of the world," said Ben, after Lambert had been pointing out some of the oddities and beauties of the suburbs—"it is all windmills. You remember his terrific contest with one, I suppose."

"No," said Lambert, bluntly.

"Well, I don't either; that is, not definitely. But there was something of that kind in his adventures, and if there wasn't, there should nave been. Look at them, how frantically they whirl their great arms—just the thing to excite the crazy knight to mortal combat. It bewilders one to look at them; help me count all those we can see, Van Mounen. I want a big item for my notebook"—and, after a careful reckoning, superintended by all the party, Master Ben wrote in pencil, "Saw, Dec. —, 184–, ninety-eight windmills within full view of Leyden."

He would have been glad to visit the old brick mill in which the painter Rembrandt was born, but he abandoned the project upon learning that it would take them out of their way. Few boys as hungry as Ben was by this time would hesitate long between Rembrandt's home, a mile off, and lunch close by. Ben chose the latter.

After lunch they rested awhile and then—took another, which, for form's sake, they called dinner. After dinner the boys sat warming themselves at the inn—all but Peter, who occupied the time in another fruitless search for Dr. Boekman.

This over, the party once more prepared for skating. They were thirteen miles from The Hague and not as fresh as when they had left Broek early on the previous day, but they were in good spirits and the ice was excellent.

As the boys skated onward they saw a number of fine country seats, all decorated and surrounded according to the Dutchest of Dutch taste, but impressive to look upon, with their great, formal houses, elaborate gardens, square hedges, and wide ditches—some crossed by a bridge having a gate in the middle to be carefully locked at night.

The boys traveled bravely, all the while performing the surprising feat of producing gingerbread from their pockets and causing it to vanish instantly.

Twelve miles were passed. A few more long strokes would take them to The Hague, when Van Mounen proposed that they should vary their course by walking into the city through the Bosch.

"Agreed!" cried one and all, and their skates were off in a twinkling.

The Bosch is a grand park or wood, nearly two miles long, containing the celebrated House in the Wood, sometimes used as a royal residence.

The park surrounding the palace is charming, especially in summer, for flowers and birds make it bright as fairyland. Long rows of magnificent oaks rear their proud heads, conscious that no profaning hand will ever bring them low. In fact, the Bosch has for ages been held as an almost sacred spot. Children are never allowed to meddle with its smallest twig; the axe of the woodman has never resounded there. Even war and riot have passed it reverently, pausing for a moment in their devastating way.

What wonder, then, that the oaks have a grand, fearless air? Birds from all Holland have told them how, elsewhere, trees are cropped and bobbed into shape—but *they* are untouched. Year after year they expand in unclipped luxuriance and beauty; their wide-spreading foliage, alive with song, casts a cool shade over lawn and pathway or bows to its image in the sunny ponds.

Even on that winter day the Bosch was beautiful. Its trees were bare, but beneath them still lay the ponds, every ripple smoothed into glass. The blue sky was bright overhead, and as it looked down through the thicket of boughs it saw another blue sky, not nearly so bright, looking up from the dim thicket under the ice.

Never had the sunset appeared more beautiful to Peter than when he saw it exchanging farewell glances with the windows and shining roofs of the city before him. Never had The Hague itself seemed more inviting. He was no longer Peter van Holp, going to visit a great city, nor a fine young gentleman bent on sight-seeing; he was a knight, an adventurer, travel-soiled and weary, a Hop-o'-My-Thumb grown large, a Fortunatus approaching the enchanted castle where luxury and ease awaited him—for his own sister's house was not half a mile away.

"At last, boys," he cried in high glee, "we may hope for a royal resting-place—good beds, warm rooms, and something to eat. Our lodgings at the Red Lion have made us appreciate our own homes."

XX

THE MERCHANT PRINCE AND THE PRINCESS

WELL might Peter feel that his sister's house was like an enchanted castle. Large and elegant as it was, a spell of quiet hung over it. The very lion crouching at its gate seemed to have been turned into stone through magic. Within, it was guarded by genii, in the shape of red-faced servants, who sprang silently forth at the summons of bell or knocker. There was a cat, also, who appeared as knowing as any Puss-in-Boots; and a brass gnome in the hall whose business it was to stand with outstretched arms ready to receive sticks and umbrellas. Safe within the walls bloomed a Garden of Delight, where the flowers firmly believed it was summer, and a sparkling fountain was laughing merrily to itself because Jack Frost could not find it. There was a Sleeping

Beauty, too, just at the time of the boys' arrival; but when Peter, like a true prince, flew lightly up the stairs and kissed her eyelids, the enchantment was broken. The princess became his own good sister and the fairy castle just one of the finest, most comfortable houses of The Hague.

As may well be believed, the boys received the heartiest of welcomes. After they had conversed awhile with their lively hostess, one of the genii summoned them to a grand repast in a red-curtained room, where floor and ceiling shone like polished ivory and the mirrors suddenly blossomed into rosy-cheeked boys as far as the eye could reach.

They had caviare now, and salmagundi, and sausage and cheese, besides salad and fruit and biscuit and cake. How the boys could partake of such a medley was a mystery to Ben; for the salad was sour, and the cake was sweet; the fruit was dainty, and the salmagundi heavy with onions and fish. But, while he was wondering, he made a hearty meal and was soon absorbed in deciding which he really preferred, the coffee or the anisette cordial. It was delightful, too—this taking one's food from dishes of frosted silver, and wine-glasses from which Titania herself might have sipped. The young gentleman afterward wrote to his mother that pretty and choice as things were at home, he had never known what cut glass, china and silver services were until he visited The Hague.

Of course Peter's sister soon heard of all the boys' adventures,—how they had skated over forty miles and seen rare sights on the way; how they had lost their purse and found it again; how one of the party had fallen and given them an excuse for a grand sail in an ice-boat; how, above all, they had caught a robber, and so for a second time saved their slippery purse.

"And now, Peter," said the lady, when the story was

finished, "you must write at once to tell the good people of Broek that your adventures have reached their height; that you and your fellow-travelers have all been taken prisoners."

The boys looked startled.

"Indeed, I shall do no such thing," laughed Peter, "we must leave tomorrow at noon."

But the sister had already decided differently, and a Holland lady is not to be easily turned from her purpose. In short, she held forth such strong temptations and was so bright and cheerful, and said so many coaxing and unanswerable things, both in English and Dutch, that the boys were all delighted when it was settled that they should remain at The Hague for at least two days.

Next, the grand skating race was talked over. Mevrouw van Gend gladly promised to be present on the occasion. "I shall witness your triumph, Peter," she said, "for you are the fastest skater I ever knew."

Peter blushed and gave a slight cough, as Carl answered for him.

"Ah, mevrouw, he is swift, but all the Broek boys are fine skaters—even the rag-pickers"—and he thought bitterly of poor Hans.

The lady laughed. "That will make the race all the more exciting," she said, "but I shall wish each of you to be the winner."

At this moment her husband, Mynheer van Gend, came in, and the enchantment falling upon the boys was complete.

The invisible fairies of the household at once clustered about them, whispering that Jasper van Gend had a heart as young and fresh as their own, and if he loved anything in this world more than industry it was sunshine and frolic.

They hinted also something about his having a heart full of love and a head full of wisdom, and finally gave the boys to understand that when Mynheer said a thing he meant it.

Therefore his frank "Well now, this is pleasant," as he shook hands with them all, made the boys feel quite at home and as happy as squirrels.

There were fine paintings in the drawing-room and exquisite statuary, and portfolios filled with rare Dutch engravings, besides many beautiful and curious things from China and Japan. The boys felt that it would require a month to examine all the treasures of the apartment.

Ben noticed with pleasure English books lying upon the table. He saw also over the carved, upright piano, life-sized portraits of William of Orange and his English queen, a sight that for a time brought England and Holland side by side in his heart.

While Ben was looking at the portraits, Mynheer van Gend was giving the boys an account of a recent visit to Antwerp.

Then, turning to Ben, the host talked with him in English of the fine old Belgian city. Among other things, he told the origin of its name. Ben had been taught that Antwerp was derived from *ae'nt werf* (on the wharf), but Mynheer van Gend gave him a far more interesting derivation.

It appears that about three thousand years ago a great giant, named Antigonus, lived on the river Scheld, on the site of the present city of Antwerp. This giant claimed half the merchandise of all navigators who passed his castle. Of course some were inclined to oppose this simple regulation. In such cases Antigonus, by way of teaching them to practice better manners next time, cut off and threw into the river the right hands of the merchants. Thus *hand-werpen* (or hand-throwing), changed to Antwerp, came to be the name of the place.

When Mynheer van Gend had related in two languages this story of Antwerp, he was tempted to tell other legends— some in English, some in Dutch; and so the moments, borne upon the swift shoulders of gnomes and giants, glided rapidly away toward bedtime.

It was hard to break up so pleasant a party, but the Van Gend household moved with the regularity of clockwork. There was no lingering at the threshold when the cordial "Good-night!" was spoken. Even while our boys were mounting the stairs the invisible household fairies again clustered around them, whispering that system and regularity had been chief builders of the master's prosperity.

Beautiful chambers with three beds in them were not to be found in this mansion. Some of the rooms contained two, but each visitor slept alone. Before morning, the motto of the party evidently was "Every boy his own chrysalis"—and Peter, at least, was not sorry to have it so.

Peter was up first the next morning; knowing the punctual habits of his brother-in-law, he took good care that none of the boys should oversleep themselves. A hard task he found it to wake Jacob Poot, but after pulling that young gentleman out of bed and with Ben's help dragging him about the room awhile, he succeeded in arousing him.

While Jacob was dressing and moaning within him, because the felt slippers provided him as a guest were too tight for his swollen feet, Peter wrote to inform their friends at Broek of the safe arrival of his party at The Hague. He

also begged his mother to send word to Hans Brinker that
Dr. Boekman had not yet reached Leyden, but that a letter
containing Hans' message had been left at the hotel where the
doctor always lodged during his visits to the city. "Tell him,
also," wrote Peter, "that I shall call there again as I pass
through Leyden. The poor boy seemed to feel sure that 'the
meester' would hasten to save his father, but we, who know
the gruff old gentleman, better, may be confident he will do
no such thing. It would be a kindness to send a visiting
physician from Amsterdam to the cottage at once, if Dame
Brinker will consent to receive any but the great king of the
meesters, as Dr. Boekman certainly is.

"You know, mother," added Peter, "that I have always
considered sister van Gend's house as rather quiet and lonely,
but I assure you it is not so now. Sister says our presence
has warmed it for the whole winter. Brother van Gend is
very kind to us all. He says we make him wish that he had
a houseful of boys of his own. He has promised to let us
ride on his noble black horses. Ludwig has given us a name
already—the Black Cavalry. We flatter ourselves that we
shall make an imposing appearance, especially in single file."

The Black Cavalry was not disappointed. Mynheer van
Gend readily procured good horses, and all the boys could
ride, though none were as perfect horsemen (or horseboys) as
Peter and Ben. They saw The Hague to their hearts' content; and The Hague saw them—expressing its approbation
loudly through the mouths of small boys and cart-dogs.

On their return, the boys pronounced the great porcelain
stove in the family sitting-room a decidedly useful piece of
furniture, for they could gather round it and get warm without burning their noses or bringing on chilblains. It was so
very large that, though hot nowhere, it seemed to send out

warmth by the houseful—its pure white sides and polished brass rings made it a pretty object to look upon, notwithstanding the fact that our ungrateful Ben, while growing thoroughly warm and comfortable beside it, concocted a satirical sentence for his next letter, to the effect that a stove in Holland must of course resemble a great tower of snow or it wouldn't be in keeping with the oddity of the country.

XXI

WHILE tramping on foot through the city, Ben often longed for a good English sidewalk. Here, as in the other towns, there was no curb, no raised pavement for foot travelers, but the streets were clean and even, and all vehicles were kept scrupulously within a certain tract. Strange to say, there were nearly as many sleds as wagons to be seen, though there was not a particle of snow. The sleds went scraping over the bricks or cobble-stones, some provided with an apparatus in front for sprinkling water, to diminish the friction, and some rendered less musical by means of a dripping oil rag, which the driver occasionally applied to the runners.

Ben was surprised at the noiseless way in which Dutch laborers do their work. Even around the warehouses and docks there was no bustle, no shouting from one to another. Entire loads of cheeses or herrings are pitched from cart or canal-boat into the warehouses without a word, but the passer-by must take his chance of being pelted, for a Dutchman seldom looks before or behind him while engaged at work.

Poor Jacob Poot, who seemed destined to bear all the mishaps of the journey, was knocked nearly breathless by a great cheese which a fat Dutchman was throwing to a fellow laborer, but he recovered himself and passed on without evincing the least indignation.

Ben professed great sympathy on the occasion, but Jacob insisted that it was "notting."

"Then why did you screw your face so when it hit you?"

"What for screw mine face?" repeated Jacob soberly, "Vy, it vash de—de——"

"The what?" insisted Ben maliciously.

"Vy, de—de—vat you call dis—vat you taste mit de nose?"

Ben laughed.

"Oh, you mean the smell."

"Yesh. Dat ish it," said Jacob eagerly—"it wash de schmell. I draw mine face for dat!"

"Ha! ha!" roared Ben, "that's a good one. A Dutch boy smell a cheese. You can never make me believe *that!*"

"Vell, it is no matter," replied Jacob, trudging on beside Ben in perfect good humor—"vait till you hit mit cheese—dat ish all."

Soon he added pathetically—"Penchamin, I no likes be call Tutch—dat ish no goot. I bees a Hollander."

Just as Ben was apologizing, Lambert hailed him:

"Hold up, Ben! Here is the Fish Market. There is not much to be seen at this season. But we can take a look at the storks if you wish."

Ben knew that storks were held in peculiar reverence in Holland and that the bird figured upon the arms of the Capital. Therefore he pressed eagerly forward as Van Mounen led the way through the Fish Market, anxious to see if storks in Holland were anything like the melancholy specimens he had seen in the Zoological Gardens of London.

Ben soon made up his mind, and rightly, too, that The Hague, with its fine streets and public parks shaded with elms, was a magnificent city. The prevailing costume was like that of London or Paris, and his British ears were many a time cheered by the music of British words.

Another thing attracted him—the milkmen's carts. These were small affairs, filled with shiny brass kettles, or stone jars, and drawn by dogs. The milkman walked meekly beside his cart keeping his dog in order and delivering the milk to customers. Certain fish dealers had dog-carts, also, and when a herring-dog chanced to meet a milk-dog, he invariably put on airs and growled as he passed him. Sometimes a milk-dog would recognize an acquaintance before another milk-cart across the street, and then, how the kettles would rattle, especially if they were empty! Each dog would give a bound and, never caring for his master's whistle, insist upon meeting the other half way. Sometimes they contented themselves with an inquisitive sniff, but, generally the smaller dog made an affectionate snap at the larger one's ear, or a friendly tussle was engaged in by way of exercise. Then, woe! to the milk-kettles, and woe! to the dogs!

The whipping over, each dog, expressing his feeling as best he could, would trot leisurely back to his work.

XXII

HOMEWARD BOUND

THE sight-seeing came to an end at last. On Monday morning, bright and early, our boys bade farewell to their kind entertainers and started on their homeward journey.

Peter lingered awhile at the lion-guarded door, for he and his sister had many parting words to say.

As Ben saw them bidding each other "good-bye," he could not help feeling that kisses as well as clocks were wonderfully alike everywhere. The English kiss that his sister Jennie gave when he left home had said the same thing to him that Vrouw van Gend's Dutch kiss said to Peter. Ludwig had taken his share of the farewell in the most matter-of-fact manner possible, and though he loved his sister well, had winced a little at her making such a child of him as to put an extra kiss "for mother" upon his forehead.

He was already upon the canal with Carl and Jacob. Were they thinking about sisters or kisses? Not a bit of it. They were so happy to be on skates once more, so impatient to dart at once into the very heart of Broek, that they spun and wheeled about like crazy fellows.

Even Lambert and Ben, who had been waiting at the street-corner, began to grow impatient.

The captain joined them at last. They were soon on the canal with the rest.

"Hurry up, Peter," growled Ludwig—"we're freezing by inches—there! I knew you'd be the last after all to get on your skates!"

"Did you?" said his brother, looking up with an air of deep interest—"clever boy!"

Ludwig laughed, but tried to look cross as he said, "I'm in earnest, anyhow. We must get home some time this year."

"Now, boys," cried Peter, springing up, as he fastened the last buckle, "there's a clear way before us! We will imagine it's the grand race. Ready! One—two—three—*start!*"

I assure you very little was said for the first half hour. They were six Mercuries skimming the ice. In plain English, they went like lightning.

After a while Jacob slackened his speed—then Ludwig—then Lambert—then Carl.

They soon halted to take a long breath and finally found themselves standing in a group gazing after Peter and Ben, who were still racing in the distance as if their lives were at stake.

"It is very evident," said Lambert, as he and his three companions started on again, "that neither of them will give up if he can help it."

"What foolishness!" growled Carl, "to tire themselves at the beginning of the journey—but they're racing in earnest, that's certain. Hello! Peter's flagging!"

"Not so!" cried Ludwig—"catch him being beaten!"

"Ha! ha!" sneered Carl. "I tell you, boy, Benjamin is ahead."

Now, if Ludwig disliked anything in this world it was to be called a boy—probably because he was nothing else. He grew indignant at once.

"Humph! what are *you*, I wonder? There, sir! *now* look and see if Peter isn't ahead!"

"*I* think he *is*," interposed Lambert, "but I can't quite tell at this distance."

"*I* think he isn't!" retorted Carl.

Jacob was growing anxious—he always abhorred an argument—so he said in a coaxing tone, "Don't quarrel—don't quarrel!"

"Don't quarrel!" mocked Carl, looking back at Jacob as he skated. "Who's quarreling? Poot, you're a goose!"

"I can't help that," was Jacob's meek reply. "See! they are nearing the turn of the canal."

"*Now* we can see!" cried Ludwig in great excitement. "Peter will make it first, I know."

"He can't—for Ben is ahead!" insisted Carl. "Gunst! That ice-boat will run over him. No! he is clear! They're a couple of geese anyhow. Hurrah! they're at the turn. Who's ahead?"

"*Peter!*" cried Ludwig joyfully.

"Good for the captain!" shouted Lambert and Jacob.

And Carl condescended to mutter:

"It *is* Peter after all. I thought, all the time, that head fellow was Ben."

This turn in the canal had evidently been their goal, for the two racers came to a sudden halt after passing it.

Carl said something about being "glad that they had sense enough to stop and rest," and the four boys skated on in silence to overtake their companions.

All the while, Carl was secretly wishing that he had kept on with Peter and Ben, as he felt sure he could easily have come out winner. He was a very rapid, though by no means a graceful skater.

Ben was looking at Peter with mingled vexation, admiration and surprise as the boys drew near:

They heard him saying in English:

"You're a perfect bird on the ice, Peter van Holp. The first fellow that ever beat me in a fair race, I can tell you!"

Peter, who understood the language better than he could speak it, returned a laughing bow at Ben's compliment, but made no further reply. Possibly he was scant of breath at the time.

"Now, Benchamin, vat you do mit yourself? get so hot as a fire-brick—dat ish no goot," was Jacob's plaintive comment.

"Nonsense!" answered Ben. "This frosty air will cool me soon enough. I am not tired."

"You are beaten, though, my boy," said Lambert in English, "and fairly, too. How will it be, I wonder, on the day of the grand race?"

Ben flushed and gave a proud, defiant laugh, as if to say:

"This was mere pastime. I'm *determined* to beat them—come what will!"

XXIII

BY the time the boys reached the village of Voorhout, which stands near the Grand Canal, about half way between The Hague and Haarlem, they were forced to hold a council. The wind, though moderate at first, had grown stronger and stronger, until at last they could hardly skate against it. The weather-vanes throughout the country had evidently entered into a conspiracy.

"No use trying to face such a blow as this," said Ludwig. "It cuts its way down a man's throat like a knife."

"Keep your mouth shut then," grunted the affable Carl, who was strong-chested as a young ox, "I'm for keeping on."

"In this case," interposed Peter, "we must consult the weakest of the party rather than the strongest."

The captain's principle was all right, but its application was not flattering to Master Ludwig; shrugging his shoulders, he retorted:

"Who's weak? Not I, for one—but the wind's stronger than any of us. I hope you'll condescend to admit that!"

"Ha! ha!" laughed Van Mounen, who could barely keep his feet, "so it is."

Just then the weather-vanes telegraphed to each other by a peculiar twitch, and in an instant the gust came. It nearly threw the strong-chested Carl; it almost strangled Jacob, and quite upset Ludwig.

"This settles the question," shouted Peter. "Off with your skates! We'll go into Voorhout."

At Voorhout they found a little inn with a big yard. The yard was well bricked and, better than all, was provided with a complete set of skittles; so our boys soon turned the detention into a frolic. The wind was troublesome even in that sheltered quarter, but they were on good standing-ground and did not mind it.

First a hearty dinner—then the game. With pins as long as their arms, and balls as big as their heads, plenty of strength left for rolling, and a clean sweep of sixty yards for the strokes—no wonder they were happy.

That night Captain Peter and his men slept soundly. No prowling robber came to disturb them; and, as they were distributed in separate rooms, they did not even have a bolster-battle in the morning.

Such a breakfast as they ate! The landlord looked frightened. When he had asked them where they "belonged," he made up his mind that the Broek people starved their children. It was a shame, "such fine young gentlemen, too!"

Fortunately the wind had tired itself out and fallen asleep in the great sea-cradle beyond the Dunes. There were signs of snow, otherwise the weather was fine.

It was mere child's play for the well-rested boys to skate to Leyden. Here they halted awhile, for Peter had an errand at the Golden Eagle. He left the city with a lightened heart; Dr. Boekman had been at the hotel, read the note containing Hans' message, and departed for Broek.

"I cannot say it was your letter sent him off so soon,"

explained the landlord, "some rich lady in Broek was taken bad very sudden and he was sent for in haste."

Peter turned pale.

"What was the name?" he asked.

"Indeed, it went in one ear and out of the other—for all I hindered it. Plague to people who can't see a traveler in comfortable lodgings, but they must whisk him off before one can breathe."

"A lady in Broek, did you say?"

"Yes," very gruffly, "any other business, young master?"

"No, mine host—except that I and my comrades here would like a bite of something and a drink of hot coffee."

"Ah," said the landlord sweetly, "a bite you shall have, and coffee, too, the finest in Leyden. Walk up to the stove, my masters—now I think again—that was a widow lady—from Rotterdam, I think they said—visiting at one Van Stoepel's, if I mistake not!"

"Ah!" said Peter, greatly relieved. "They live in the white house by the Schlossen Mill—now, mynheer, the coffee, please!"

"What a goose I was," thought he, as the party left the Golden Eagle, "to feel so sure it was my mother—but she may be somebody's mother, poor woman, for all that. Who can she be, I wonder?"

There were not many upon the canal that day, between Leyden and Haarlem. However, as the boys neared Amsterdam they found themselves once more in the midst of a moving throng.

"Three cheers for home!" cried Van Mounen, as they came in sight of the great Western Dock (Westelijk Dok). "Hurrah! Hurrah!" shouted one and all, "Hurrah! Hurrah!"

The Y was crossed. They were on the Broek Canal.

Lambert's home was reached first.

"Good-bye, boys!" he cried, as he left them, "we've had the greatest frolic ever known in Holland."

"So we have. Good-bye, Van Mounen!" answered the boys. "Good-bye!"

Peter hailed him. "I say, Van Mounen, the classes begin tomorrow!"

"I know it. Our holiday is over. Good-bye, again." "Good-bye!"

Broek came in sight. Such meetings! Katrinka was on the canal! Carl was delighted. Hilda was there! Peter felt rested in an instant. Rychie was there! Ludwig and Jacob nearly knocked each other over in their eagerness to shake hands with her.

Dutch girls are modest and generally quiet, but they have very glad eyes. For a few moments it was hard to decide whether Hilda, Rychie or Katrinka felt the most happy.

Annie Bouman was also on the canal, looking even prettier than the other maidens, in her graceful peasant's costume. But she did not mingle with Rychie's party, neither did she look unusually happy.

The one she liked most to see was not among the newcomers. Indeed, he was not upon the canal at all. She had not been near Broek before, since the Eve of Saint Nicholas, for she was staying with her sick grandmother in Amsterdam and had been granted a brief resting-spell, as the grandmother called it, because she had been such a faithful little nurse night and day.

Annie had devoted her resting-spell to skating with all her might toward Broek and back again, in the hope of meeting her mother or some of her family on the canal, or, it might

"WHERE CAN GRETEL BE?" THOUGHT ANNIE,
AS SHE FLEW OVER THE ICE.

be, Gretel Brinker. Not one of them had she seen, and she must hurry back without even catching a glimpse of her mother's cottage, for the poor, helpless grandmother, she knew, was by this time moaning for some one to turn her upon her cot.

"Where can Gretel be?" thought Annie, as she flew over the ice; "she can almost always steal a few moments from her work at this time of day—poor Gretel—what a dreadful thing it must be to have a dull father—I should be wofully afraid of him, I know—so strong, and yet so strange!"

Annie had not heard of his illness. Dame Brinker and her affairs received but little notice from the people of the place.

If Gretel had not been known as a goose-girl she might have had more friends among the peasantry of the neighborhood. As it was, Annie Bouman was the only one who did not feel ashamed to avow herself by word and deed the companion of Hans and Gretel.

When the neighbors' children laughed at her for keeping such poor company, she would simply flush when Hans was ridiculed, or laugh in a careless, disdainful way; but to hear little Gretel abused always awakened her wrath.

"Goose-girl, indeed!" she would say. "I can tell you any of you are fitter for the work than she. My father often said last summer that it troubled him to see such a bright-eyed, patient little maiden tending geese. Humph! She would not harm them, as you would, Janzoon Kolp; and she would not tread upon them, as you might, Kate Wouters."

This would be pretty sure to start a laugh at the clumsy, ill-natured Kate's expense, and Annie would walk loftily away from the group of young gossips. Perhaps some memory of Gretel's assailants crossed her mind as she skated rapidly toward Amsterdam, for her eyes sparkled ominously and she more than

once gave her pretty head a defiant toss. When that mood
passed, such a bright, rosy, affectionate look illumined her face
that more than one weary workingman turned to gaze after
her and to wish that he had a glad, contented lass like that
for a daughter.

There were five joyous households in Broek that night.

The boys were back safe and sound, and they found all
well at home. Even the sick lady at neighbor Van Stoepel's
was out of danger.

But the next morning! Ah, how stupidly school-bells will
ding-dong! ding-dong! when one is tired.

Ludwig was sure he had never listened to anything so
odious. Even Peter felt pathetic on the occasion. Carl said it
was a shame for a fellow to have to turn out when his bones
were splitting—and Jacob soberly bade Ben "Goot-pye!" and
walked off with his satchel as if it weighed a hundred pounds.

XXIV

THE CRISIS

WHILE the boys are nursing their fatigue, we will take a peep into the Brinker cottage.

Can it be that Gretel and her mother have not stirred since we saw them last, that the sick man upon the bed has not even turned over? It was four days ago and there is the sad group just as it was before. No, not precisely the same, for Raff Brinker is paler; his fever is gone, though he knows nothing of what is passing. Then they were alone in the bare room. Now there is another group in an opposite corner.

Dr. Boekman is there, talking in a low tone with a stout young man who listens intently. The stout young man is his student and assistant. Hans is there also. He stands near the window, respectfully waiting until he shall be accosted.

"You see, Vollenhoven, it is probably like Rip Donderdunck's case," Dr. Boekman said, in a low, mumbling tone. "He fell from the top of Voppelploot's windmill. After the accident the man was stupid, and finally became idiotic. In time he lay helpless like yon fellow on the bed; moaned, too, like him, and kept constantly lifting his hand to his head. My learned friend Van Choppem performed an operation upon this Donderdunck and discovered under the skull a small dark sac, which pressed upon the brain. This had been the cause of the trouble. My friend Van Choppem removed it—a splendid operation!"

"Did the man live?" asked the assistant, respectfully.

Dr. Boekman scowled. "That is of no consequence. I believe he died, but why not fix your mind on the grand features of the case?"

"But, mynheer," gently persisted the student, who knew that the doctor would discuss the case for hours unless pulled at once from this subject,—"Mynheer, you have other engagements today—three legs in Amsterdam, you remember, an eye in Broek, and that tumor up the canal."

"The tumor can wait," said the doctor reflectively. "That is another beautiful case—a beautiful case! The woman has not lifted her head from her shoulder for two months—magnificent tumor, sir!"

The doctor by this time was speaking aloud. He had quite forgotten where he was.

Vollenhoven made another attempt.

"This poor fellow on the bed, mynheer. Do you think you can save him?"

"Ah, indeed, certainly," stammered the doctor, suddenly, perceiving that he had been talking rather off the point—"certainly, that is—I hope so——"

"If anyone in Holland can, mynheer," murmured the assistant with honest bluntness—"it is yourself."

The doctor looked displeased—growled out a tender request for the student to talk less, and beckoned Hans to draw near.

This strange man had a great horror of speaking to women, especially on surgical matters. "One can never tell," he said, "what moment the creatures will scream or faint." Therefore he explained Raff Brinker's case to Hans and told him what he believed should be done to save the patient.

Hans listened attentively, growing red and pale by turns, and throwing quick, anxious glances toward the bed.

"It may *kill* the father—did you say, mynheer?" he exclaimed at last, in a trembling whisper.

"It may, my boy. But I have a strong belief that it will cure and not kill. Ah! if boys were not such dunces, I could lay the whole matter before you, but it would be of no use."

Hans looked blank at this compliment.

"It would be of no use," repeated Doctor Boekman indignantly; "a great operation is proposed—but one might as well do it with a hatchet. The only question asked is—'will it kill?'"

"The question is *everything* to us, mynheer," said Hans, with tearful dignity.

Doctor Boekman looked at him in sudden dismay.

"Ah! exactly so. You are right, boy, I am a fool. Good boy. One does not wish one's father killed—of course not. I am a fool."

"Will he die, mynheer, if this sickness goes on?"

"Humph! this is no new illness. The same thing growing worse every instant—pressure on the brain—will take him off soon like *that*," said the doctor, snapping his fingers.

"And the operation *may* save him," pursued Hans. "How soon, mynheer, can we know?"

Doctor Boekman grew impatient.

"In a day, perhaps an hour. Talk with your mother, boy, and let her decide. My time is short."

Hans approached his mother; at first, when she looked up at him, he could not utter a syllable; then, turning his eyes away, he said in a firm voice:

"I must speak with the mother alone."

Quick little Gretel, who could not quite understand what was passing, threw rather an indignant look at Hans and walked away.

"Come back, Gretel, and sit down," said Hans sorrowfully. She obeyed.

Dame Brinker and her boy stood by the window while the doctor and his assistant, bending over the bedside, conversed together in a low tone. There was no danger of disturbing the patient. He appeared like one blind and deaf. Only his faint, piteous moans showed him to be a living man. Hans was talking earnestly, and in a low voice, for he did not wish his sister to hear.

With dry, parted lips, Dame Brinker leaned toward him, searching his face, as if suspecting a meaning beyond his words. Once she gave a quick, frightened sob that made Gretel start, but after that listened calmly.

When Hans ceased to speak, his mother turned, gave one long, agonized look at her husband, lying there so pale and unconscious, and threw herself on her knees beside the bed.

Poor little Gretel! What did all this mean? She looked with questioning eyes at Hans. He was standing, but his head was bent as if in prayer;—at the doctor, he was gently feeling her father's head and looked like one examining some curious stone;—at the assistant, the man coughed and turned away;—at her mother. Ah! little Gretel, that was the best you could do—to kneel beside her and twine your warm young arms about her neck—to weep and implore God to listen.

When the mother arose, Doctor Boekman, with a show of trouble in his eyes, asked gruffly, "Well, jufvrouw, shall it be done?"

"Will it pain him, mynheer?" she asked in a trembling voice.

"I cannot say. Probably not. Shall it be done?"

"It may *cure* him, you said, and—mynheer, did you tell my boy that—perhaps—perhaps"—she could not finish.

"Yes, jufvrouw, I said the patient might sink under the operation—but we will hope it may prove otherwise"—(he looked at his watch. The assistant moved impatiently toward the window.) "Come, jufvrouw, time presses. Yes or no?"

Hans wound his arm about his mother. It was not his usual way. He even leaned his head against her shoulder.

"The meester awaits an answer," he whispered.

Dame Brinker had long been the head of her house in every sense. Many a time she had been very stern with Hans, ruling him with a strong hand and rejoicing in her motherly discipline—*now* she felt so weak, so helpless. It was something to feel that firm embrace. There was strength even in the touch of that yellow hair.

She turned to her boy imploringly.

"Oh, Hans! what shall I say?"

"Say what God tells thee, mother," answered Hans, bowing his head.

One quick, questioning prayer to Heaven rose from the mother's heart. The answer came.

She turned toward Doctor Boekman.

"It is right, mynheer. I consent."

"Humph!" grunted the doctor, as if to say, "You've been long enough about it." Then he conferred a moment with his assistant, who listened with great outward deference but was inwardly rejoicing at the grand joke he would have to tell his fellow students. He had actually seen a tear in "old Boekman's" eye.

Meanwhile Gretel looked on in trembling silence, but when she saw the doctor open a leathern case and take out one sharp, gleaming instrument after another, she sprang forward.

"Oh, mother—the poor father meant no wrong. Are they going to *murder* him?"

"I do not know, child," screamed Dame Brinker, looking fiercely at Gretel—"*I do not know!*"

"This will not do, jufvrouw," said Doctor Boekman sternly, and at the same time he cast a quick, penetrating look at Hans—"you and the girl must leave the room. The boy may stay."

Dame Brinker drew herself up in an instant. Her eyes flashed. Her whole countenance was changed. She looked like one who had never wept, never felt a woman's weakness. Her voice was low but decided. "I stay with my husband, mynheer."

Dr. Boekman looked astonished. His orders were seldom disregarded in this style. For an instant his eye met hers.

"You may remain, jufvrouw," he said in an altered voice.

Gretel had already disappeared.

In one corner of the cottage was a small closet where her rough, box-like bed was fastened against the wall: none would think of the trembling little creature crouching there in the dark.

Doctor Boekman took off his heavy coat; he filled an earthen basin with water and placed it near the bed. Then, turning to Hans, he asked:

"Can I depend upon you, boy?"

"You can, mynheer."

"I believe you. Stand at the head here—your mother may sit at your right—so," and he placed a chair near the cot.

"Remember, jufvrouw, there must be no cries, no fainting."
Dame Brinker answered him with a look.

He was satisfied.

"Now, Vollenhoven."

Oh! that case with the terrible instruments. The assistant lifted them. Gretel, who had been peering, with brimming eyes, through the crack of the closet door, could remain silent no longer.

She rushed frantically across the apartment, seized her hood, and ran from the cottage.

XXV

GRETEL AND HILDA

IT was the recess hour. At the first stroke of the school-house bell the canal seemed to give a tremendous shout and grow suddenly alive with boys and girls.

Dozens of gaily clad children were skating in and out among each other, and all their pent-up merriment of the morning was relieving itself in song and shout and laughter. There was nothing to check the flow of frolic. Not a thought of school-books came out with them into the sunshine. Latin, arithmetic, grammar—all were locked up for an hour in the dingy school-room. The teacher might be a noun if he wished, and a proper one at that, but *they* meant to enjoy themselves. As long as the skating was as perfect as this it made no difference whether Holland were on the North Pole or the Equator.

In the height of the fun one of the children called out: "What is that?"

"What? Where?" cried a dozen voices.

"Why—don't you see? That dark thing over there by the idiot's cottage."

"I don't see anything," said one.

"I do," shouted another, "it's a dog!"

"Where's any dog?" put in a squeaky voice that we have heard before—"it's no such thing—it's a heap of rags."

147

"Pooh! Voost," retorted another, gruffly, "that's about as near the fact as you ever get—it's the goose-girl, Gretel, looking for rats."

"Well, what of it?" squeaked Voost, "isn't *she* a bundle of rags, I'd like to know?"

"Ha! ha! Pretty good for you, Voost! You'll get a medal for wit yet, if you keep on."

"You'd get something else, if her brother Hans were here. I'll warrant you would!" said a muffled up little fellow, with a cold in his head.

As Hans was *not* there, Voost could afford to scout the insinuation.

"Who cares for *him,* little sneezer? I'd fight a dozen like him any day, and you in the bargain."

"You would! would you? I'd like to catch you at it," and, by way of proving his words, the sneezer skated off at the top of his speed.

Just then a general chase after three of the biggest boys of the school was proposed—and friend and foe, frolicsome as ever, were soon united in a common cause.

Only one of all that happy throng remembered the dark little form by the idiot's cottage. Poor, frightened Gretel! She was not thinking of them, though their merry laughter floated lightly toward her, making her feel like one in a dream.

How loud the moans were behind the darkened window— what if those strange men were really killing her father!

The thought made her spring to her feet with a cry of horror!

"Ah! no," she sobbed, sinking upon the frozen mound of earth where she had been sitting, "mother is there, and Hans. They will care for him. But how pale they were. And even Hans was crying!

"Why did the cross old meester keep *him,* and send me away," she thought; "I could have clung to the mother and kissed her. That always makes her stroke my hair and speak gently, even after she has scolded me! How quiet it is now! Oh, if the father should die, and Hans, and the mother, what *would* I do?" and Gretel, shivering with cold, buried her face in her arms and cried as if her heart would break.

The poor child had been tasked beyond her strength during the past four days. Through all she had been her mother's willing little handmaiden, soothing, helping and cheering the half-widowed woman by day and watching and praying beside her all the long night. She knew that something terrible and mysterious was taking place at this moment, something that had been too terrible and mysterious for even kind, good Hans to tell.

Then new thoughts came. Why had not Hans told her? It was a shame. It was *her* father as well as his. She was no baby. She had once taken a sharp knife from the father's hand. She had even drawn him away from the mother on that awful night when Hans, big as he was, could not help her. Why, then, must she be treated like one who could do nothing? Oh, how very still it was—how bitter, bitter cold! If Annie Bouman had only stayed home instead of going to Amsterdam it wouldn't be so lonely. How cold her feet were growing—was it the moaning that made her feel as if she were floating in the air?

This would not do—the mother might need her help at any moment!

Rousing herself with an effort, Gretel sat upright, rubbing her eyes and wondering—wondering that the sky was so bright and blue—wondering at the stillness in the cottage— more than all, at the laughter rising and falling in the distance.

Soon she sank down again, the strange medley of thought growing more and more confused in her bewildered brain.

A firm hand was laid upon her shoulder

"Get up, little girl!" cried a kind voice. "This will not do, for you to lie here and freeze."

Gretel slowly raised her head. She was so sleepy that it seemed nothing strange to her that Hilda van Gleck should be leaning over her, looking with kind, beautiful eyes into her face. She had often dreamed it before.

But she had never dreamed that Hilda was shaking her roughly, almost dragging her by main force—never dreamed that she heard her saying, "Gretel! Gretel Brinker! you *must* wake!"

This was real. Gretel looked up. Still the lovely, delicate young lady was shaking, rubbing, fairly pounding her. Her hands were tingling, her feet throbbing—Hilda was forcing her to walk.

At last Gretel began to feel like herself again.

"I have been asleep," she faltered, rubbing her eyes with both hands and looking very much ashamed.

"Yes, indeed, entirely too much asleep," laughed Hilda, whose lips were very pale, "but you are well enough now— lean upon me, Gretel; there, keep moving—you will soon be warm enough to go by the fire—now let me take you into the cottage."

"Oh, no! no! no! jufvrouw, not in there! the meester is there. He sent me away!"

Hilda was puzzled, but she wisely forebore to ask at present for an explanation. "Very well, Gretel—try to walk faster—I saw you upon the mound some time ago, but I thought you were playing—that is right—keep moving."

All this time the kind-hearted girl had been forcing Gretel to walk up and down, supporting her with one arm and with the other striving as well as she could to take off her warm sacque.

Suddenly Gretel suspected her intention.

"Oh, jufvrouw! jufvrouw!" she cried imploringly. "*Please* never think of such a thing as *that*—oh! please keep it on, I am burning all over, jufvrouw! I really am burning—not burning exactly—but pins and needles pricking all over me—oh! jufvrouw, don't."

The poor child's dismay was so genuine that Hilda hastened to reassure her.

"Very well, Gretel, move your arms then—so. Why, your cheeks are as pink as roses already. I think the meester would let you in now—he certainly would—is your father so very ill?"

"Ah, jufvrouw," cried Gretel, weeping afresh, "he is dying, I think. There are two meesters in with him at this moment and the mother has scarce spoken today. Can you hear him moan, jufvrouw?" she added, with sudden terror, "the air buzzes so I cannot hear. He may be dead! Oh, I do wish I could hear him!"

Hilda listened—the cottage was very near, but not a sound could be heard.

Something told her that Gretel was right. She ran to the window.

"You cannot see there, my lady," sobbed Gretel eagerly, "the mother has oiled paper hanging inside. But at the other one, in the south end of the cottage, you can look in where the paper is torn."

Hilda in her anxiety ran round past the corner where the low roof was fringed with its loosened thatch.

A sudden thought checked her.

"It is not right for me to peep into another's house in this way," she said to herself—then softly calling to Gretel, she added in a whisper, "You may look—perhaps he is only sleeping."

Gretel tried to walk briskly toward the spot, but her limbs were trembling. Hilda hastened to her support.

"You are sick yourself, I fear," she said kindly.

"No, not sick, jufvrouw—but my heart cries all the time now, even when my eyes are as dry as yours—why! jufvrouw, your eyes are not dry! Are you crying for *us?* Oh, jufvrouw—if God sees you! Oh! I know father will get better now"—and the little creature, even while reaching to look through the tiny window kissed Hilda's hand again and again.

The sash was sadly patched and broken, a torn piece of paper hung half way down across it. Gretel's face was pressed to the window.

"Can you see anything?" whispered Hilda at last.

"Yes—the father lies very still, his head is bandaged and all their eyes are fastened upon him. "Oh, jufvrouw!" almost screamed Gretel, as she started back and by a quick, dexterous movement shook off her heavy wooden shoes, "I *must* go in to my mother! Will you come with me?"

"Not now, the bell is ringing; I shall come again soon. Good-bye!"

Gretel scarce heard the words. She remembered for many a day afterward the bright, pitying smile on Hilda's face as she turned away.

XXVI

THE AWAKENING

AN angel could not have entered the cottage more noise-lessly. Gretel, not daring to look at anyone, slid softly to her mother's side.

The room was very still. She could hear the old doctor breathe. She could almost hear the sparks as they fell into the ashes on the hearth. The mother's hand was very cold, but a burning spot glowed on her cheek, and her eyes were like a deer's—so bright, so sad, so eager.

At last there was a movement upon the bed, very slight, but enough to cause them all to start; Dr. Boekman leaned eagerly forward.

Another movement. The large hand, so white and soft for a poor man's hand, twitched—then raised itself steadily toward the forehead.

It felt the bandage, not in a restless, crazy way, but with a questioning movement that caused even Doctor Boekman to hold his breath. Then the eyes opened slowly.

"Steady! steady!" said a voice that sounded very strange to Gretel. "Shift that mat higher, boys! Now throw on the clay. The waters are rising fast—no time to——"

Dame Brinker sprang forward like a young panther.

She seized his hands and, leaning over him, cried, "Raff! Raff, boy, speak to me!"

"Is it you, Meitje?" he asked faintly—"I have been asleep, hurt, I think—where is little Hans?"

"Here I am, father!" shouted Hans, half mad with joy. But the doctor held him back.

"He knows us!" screamed Dame Brinker. "Great God! he knows us! Gretel! Gretel! come, see your father!"

In vain Doctor Boekman commanded "Silence" and tried to force them from the bedside. He could not keep them off.

Hans and his mother laughed and cried together as they hung over the newly awakened man. Gretel made no sound, but gazed at them all with glad, startled eyes. Her father was speaking in a faint voice.

"Is the baby asleep, Meitje?"

"The baby!" echoed Dame Brinker. "Oh, Gretel! that is you! And he calls Hans 'little Hans.' Ten years asleep! Oh, mynheer, you have saved us all. He has known nothing for ten years! Children, why don't you thank the meester?"

The good woman was beside herself with joy. Doctor Boekman said nothing, but as his eye met hers he pointed upward. She understood. So did Hans and Gretel.

With one accord they knelt by the cot, side by side. Dame Brinker felt for her husband's hand even while she was praying. Doctor Boekman's head was bowed; the assistant stood by the hearth with his back toward them.

"Why do you pray?" murmured the father, looking feebly from the bed as they rose. "Is it God's day?"

It was not Sunday, but his vrouw bowed her head—she could not speak.

"Then we should have a chapter," said Raff Brinker, speaking slowly and with difficulty. "I do not know how it is. I am very, very weak. Mayhap the minister will read to us."

Gretel lifted the big Dutch Bible from its carved shelf. Doctor Boekman, rather dismayed at being called a minister, coughed and handed the volume to his assistant.

"Read," he muttered, "these people must be kept quiet or the man will die yet."

When the chapter was finished Dame Brinker motioned mysteriously to the rest by way of telling them that her husband was asleep.

"Now, jufvrouw," said the doctor in a subdued tone, as he drew on his thick woolen mittens, "there must be perfect quiet, you understand. This is truly a most remarkable case. I shall come again tomorrow. Give the patient no food today," and, bowing hastily, he left the cottage, followed by his assistant.

His grand coach was not far away; the driver had kept the horses moving slowly up and down by the canal, nearly all the time the doctor had been in the cottage.

Hans went out also.

"May God bless you, mynheer!" he said, blushing and trembling, "I can never repay you, but if——"

"Yes, you can," interrupted the doctor crossly. "You can use your wits when the patient wakes again. This clacking and snivelling is enough to kill a well man, let alone

one lying on the edge of his grave. If you want your father to get well, keep 'em quiet."

So saying, Doctor Boekman, without another word, stalked off to meet the coach, leaving Hans standing there with eyes and mouth wide open.

———

Hilda was reprimanded severely that day for returning late to school after recess and for imperfect recitations.

She had remained near the cottage until she heard Dame Brinker laugh, until she had heard Hans say, "Here I am, father!" and then she had gone back to her lessons. What wonder that she missed them! How could she get a long string of Latin verbs by heart when her heart did not care a fig for them, but would keep saying to itself, "Oh, I am so glad! I am so glad!"

XXVII

BONES AND TONGUES

BONES are strange things. One would suppose that they knew nothing at all about school affairs, but they do. Even Jacob Poot's bones, buried as they were in flesh, were sharp in the matter of study hours.

Early on the morning of his return they ached through and through, giving Jacob a twinge at every stroke of the school-bell—as if to say, "Stop that clapper! There's trouble in it." After school, on the contrary, they were quiet and comfortable; in fact, seemed to be taking a nap among their cushions.

The other boys' bones behaved in a similar manner—but that is not so remarkable. Being nearer the daylight than Jacob's, they might be expected to be more learned in the ways of the world. Master Ludwig's, especially, were like beauty, only skin deep; they were the most knowing bones you ever heard of. Just put before him ever so quietly a grammar-book with a long lesson marked in it, and immediately the sly bone over his eyes would set up such an aching! Request him to go to the garret for your foot-stove—instantly the bones would remind him that he was "too tired." Ask him to go to the confectioner's, a mile away, and *presto!* not a bone would remember that it ever had been used before.

Bearing all this in mind you will not wonder when I

tell you that our five boys were among the happiest of the happy throng pouring forth from the school-house that day.

Peter was in excellent spirits. He had heard through Hilda of Dame Brinker's laugh and of Hans' joyous words, and he needed no further proof that Raff Brinker was a cured man. In fact, the news had gone forth in every direction for miles around. Persons who had never before cared for the Brinkers, or even mentioned them, except with a contemptuous sneer or a shrug of pretended pity, now became singularly familiar with every point of their history. There was no end to the number of ridiculous stories that were flying about.

Hilda, in the excitement of the moment, had stopped to exchange a word with the doctor's coachman, as he stood by the horses, pommelling his chest and clapping his hands. Her kind heart was overflowing. She could not help pausing to tell the cold, tired-looking man that she thought the doctor would be out soon; she even hinted to him that she suspected— only suspected—that a wonderful cure had been performed— an idiot brought to his senses. Nay, she was *sure* of it—for she had heard his widow laugh—no, not his widow, of course, but his wife—for the man was as much alive as anybody, and, for all she knew, sitting up and talking like a lawyer.

All this was very indiscreet. Hilda in an impenitent sort of way felt it to be so.

But it is so delightful to impart pleasant or surprising news!

She went tripping along by the canal, quite resolved to repeat the sin, *ad infinitum,* and tell nearly every girl and boy in the school.

Meantime, Janzoon Kolp came skating by. Of course, in two seconds he was striking slippery attitudes and shouting saucy things to the coachman, who stared at him in indolent disdain

This, to Janzoon, was equivalent to an invitation to draw nearer. The coachman was now upon his box gathering up the reins and grumbling at his horses.

Janzoon accosted him.

"I say—what's going on at the idiot's cottage? Is your boss in there?"

Coachman nodded mysteriously.

"Whew!" whistled Janzoon, drawing closer, "Old Brinker dead?"

The driver grew big with importance and silent in proportion.

"See here, old pincushion, I'd run home yonder and get you a chunk of gingerbread if I thought you could open your mouth."

Old pincushion was human—long hours of waiting had made him ravenously hungry. At Janzoon's hint his countenance showed signs of a collapse.

"That's right, old fellow," pursued his tempter, "hurry up—what news—old Brinker dead?"

"No—*cured!* got his wits," said the coachman, shooting forth his words one at a time like so many bullets.

Like bullets (figuratively speaking) they hit Janzoon Kolp. He jumped as if he had been shot.

"Goede Gunst! you don't say so!"

The man pressed his lips together and looked significantly toward Master Kolp's shabby residence.

Just then Janzoon saw a group of boys in the distance. Hailing them in a rowdy style, common to boys of his stamp all over the world, whether in Africa, Japan, Amsterdam or

Paris—he scampered toward them, forgetting coachman, gingerbread, everything but the wonderful news.

Therefore by sundown it was well known throughout the neighboring country that Doctor Boekman, chancing to stop at the cottage, had given the idiot Brinker a tremendous dose of medicine, as brown as gingerbread. It had taken six men to hold him while it was poured down. The idiot had immediately sprung to his feet, in full possession of all his faculties—knocked over the doctor, or thrashed him (there was admitted to be a slight uncertainty as to which of these penalties was inflicted), then sat down and addressed him for all the world like a lawyer. After that he had turned and spoken beautifully to his wife and children. Dame Brinker had laughed herself into violent hysterics. Hans had said, "Here I am, father! your own dear son," and Gretel had said, "Here I am, father, your own dear Gretel!" and the doctor had afterward been seen leaning back in his carriage looking just as white as a corpse.

XXVIII

A NEW ALARM

WHEN Doctor Boekman called the next day at the Brinker cottage he could not help noticing the cheerful, comfortable aspect of the place. An atmosphere of happiness breathed upon him as he opened the door. Dame Brinker sat complacently knitting beside the bed, her husband was enjoying a tranquil slumber, and Gretel was noiselessly kneading rye bread on the table in the corner.

The doctor did not remain long. He asked a few simple questions, appeared satisfied with the answers, and after feeling his patient's pulse said—"Ah, very weak yet, jufvrouw; very weak, indeed. He must have nourishment. You may begin to feed the patient, ahem! not too much, but what you do give him let it be strong and of the best."

"Black bread we have, mynheer, and porridge," replied Dame Brinker cheerily, "they have always agreed with him well."

"Tut! tut!" said the doctor, frowning, "nothing of the kind. He must have the juice of fresh meat, white bread, dried and toasted, good Malaga wine, and—ahem! The man looks cold—give him more covering, something light and warm. Where is the boy?"

"Hans, mynheer, has gone into Broek to look for work. He will be back soon. Will the meester please be seated?"

Whether the hard, polished stool offered by Dame Brinker did not look particularly tempting, or whether the dame herself frightened him, partly because she was a woman, and partly because an anxious, distressed look had suddenly appeared in her face, I cannot say. Certain it is that our eccentric doctor looked hurriedly about him, muttered something about "extraordinary case," bowed, and disappeared, before Dame Brinker had time to say another word.

Strange that the visit of their good benefactor should have left a cloud, yet so it was. Gretel frowned, an anxious, childish frown, and kneaded the bread-dough violently, without looking up. Dame Brinker hurried to her husband's bedside, leaned over him, and fell into silent but passionate weeping.

In a moment Hans entered.

"Why, mother," he whispered in alarm, "what ails thee? Is the father worse?"

She turned her quivering face toward him, making no attempt to conceal her distress.

"Yes. He is starving—perishing. The meester said it."

Hans turned pale.

"What does this mean, mother? We must feed him at once. Here, Gretel, give me the porridge."

"Nay!" cried the mother distractedly, yet without raising her voice, "it may kill him. Our poor fare is too heavy for him. Oh, Hans, he will die—the father will *die* if we use him this way. He must have meat, and sweet wine, and a dekbed. Oh, what shall I do? what shall I do?" she sobbed, wringing her hands. "There is not a dollar in the house."

Gretel pouted; it was the only way she could express sympathy just then; her tears fell one by one into the dough.

"Did the meester say he *must* have these things, mother?" asked Hans.

"Yes, he did."

"Well, mother, don't cry, *he shall have them;* I shall bring meat and wine before night. Take the cover from my bed—I can sleep in the straw."

"Yes, Hans; but it is heavy, scant as it is. The meester said he must have something light and warm. He will perish. Our peat is giving out, Hans. The father has wasted it sorely, throwing it on when I was not looking, dear man."

"Never mind, mother," whispered Hans cheerfully. "We can cut down the willow tree and burn it, if need be; but I'll bring home something tonight. There *must* be work in Amsterdam, though there's none in Broek. Never fear, mother; the worst trouble of all is past. We can brave anything now that the father is himself again."

"Aye!" sobbed Dame Brinker, hastily drying her eyes, "that is true indeed."

"Of course it is. Look at him, mother, how softly he sleeps. Do you think God would let him starve, just after giving him back to us. Why, mother, I'm as *sure* of getting all the father needs as if my pocket were bursting with gold. There, now, don't fret." And hurriedly kissing her, Hans caught up his skates and slipped from the cottage.

Poor Hans! Disappointed in his morning's errand, half sickened with this new trouble, he wore a brave look and tried to whistle as he tramped resolutely off with the firm intention of mending matters.

Want had never before pressed as sorely upon the Brinker family. Their stock of peat was nearly exhausted and all the flour in the cottage was in Gretel's dough. They had scarcely cared to eat during the past few days—scarcely realized their condition. Dame Brinker had felt so sure that she and the children could earn money before the worst came that she had given herself up to the joy of her husband's recovery. She had not even told Hans that the few pieces of silver in the old mitten were quite gone.

Hans reproached himself, now, that he had not hailed the doctor when he saw him enter his coach and drive rapidly away in the direction of Amsterdam.

"Perhaps there is some mistake," he thought. "The meester surely would have known that meat and sweet wine were not at our command; and yet the father looks very weak—he certainly does. I *must* get work. If Mynheer van Holp were back from Rotterdam I could get plenty to do. But Master Peter told me to let him know if he could do aught to serve us. I shall go to him at once. Oh, if it were but summer!"

All this time Hans was hastening towards the canal. Soon his skates were on and he was skimming rapidly toward the residence of Mynheer van Holp.

"The father must have meat and wine at once," he muttered, "but how can I earn the money in time to buy them today. There is no other way but to go, as I *promised,* to Master Peter. What would a gift of meat and wine be to him? When the father is once fed, I can rush down to Amsterdam and earn the morrow's supply."

Then came other thoughts—thoughts that made his heart thump heavily and his cheeks burn with a new shame—"It is *begging,* to say the least. Not one of the Brinkers has ever been a beggar. Shall I be the first? Shall my poor father just coming back into life learn that his family have asked for charity—he, always so wise and thrifty? No," cried Hans aloud, "better a thousand times to part with the watch."

"I can at least borrow money on it in Amsterdam," he thought, turning around. "That will be no disgrace. I can find work at once and get it back again. Nay, perhaps I can even *speak to the father about it!"*

This last thought almost made the lad dance for joy. Why not, indeed, speak to the father? He was a rational being now. "He may wake," thought Hans, "quite bright and rested—may tell us the watch is of no consequence, to sell it, of course! Huzza!" and Hans almost flew over the ice.

A few moments more and the skates were again swinging from his arm. He was running towards the cottage.

His mother met him at the door.

"Oh, Hans!" she cried, her face radiant with joy, "the young lady has been here with her maid. She brought everything—meat, jelly, wine and bread—a whole basketful! Then the meester sent a man from town with more wine, and a fine bed and blankets for the father. Oh! he will get well now. God bless them!"

"God bless them!" echoed Hans, and for the first time that day, his eyes filled with tears.

XXIX

THE FATHER'S RETURN

THAT evening Raff Brinker felt so much better that he
insisted upon sitting up awhile on the rough, high-backed
chair by the fire. For a few moments there was quite a commotion in the little cottage. Hans was all-important on the
occasion, for his father was a heavy man and needed something firm to lean upon. The dame, though none of your
fragile ladies, was in such a state of alarm and excitement at
the bold step they were taking in lifting him without the
meester's orders that she came near pulling her husband over,
even while she believed herself to be his main prop and support.

"Steady, vrouw, steady!" panted Raff, "have I grown old
and feeble, or is it the fever makes me thus helpless?"

"Hear the man!" laughed Dame Brinker, "talking like

166

any other Christian. Why, you're weak from the fever, Raff. Here's the chair, all fixed snug and warm; now, sit thee down—hi-di-didy—there we are!"

With these words Dame Brinker let her half of the burden settle slowly into the chair. Hans prudently did the same.

Meanwhile Gretel flew about generally, bringing every possible thing to her mother to tuck behind the father's back and spread over his knees. Then she twitched the carved bench under his feet, and Hans kicked the fire to make it brighter.

The father was "sitting up" at last. What wonder that he looked about him like one bewildered. "Little Hans" had just been almost carrying him. "The baby" was over four feet long and was demurely brushing up the hearth with a bundle of willow wisps. Meitje, the vrouw, winsome and fair as ever, had gained at least fifty pounds in what seemed to him a few hours. She also had some new lines in her face that puzzled him. The only familiar things in the room were the pine table that he had made before he was married, the Bible upon the shelf, and the cupboard in the corner.

Ah! Raff Brinker, it was only natural that your eyes should fill with hot tears even while looking at the joyful faces of your loved ones. Ten years dropped from a man's life are no small loss; ten years of manhood, of household happiness and care; ten years of honest labor, of conscious enjoyment of sunshine and outdoor beauty, ten years of grateful life—one day looking forward to all this; the next, waking, to find them passed, and a blank. What wonder the scalding tears dropped one by one upon your cheek!

Tender little Gretel! The prayer of her life was answered through those tears. She *loved* her father from that moment.

Hans and his mother glanced silently at each other when they saw her spring towards him and throw her arms about his neck."

"Father, *dear* father," she whispered, pressing her cheek close to his, "don't cry. We are all here."

"God bless thee," sobbed Raff, kissing her again and again, "I had forgotten that!"

Soon he looked up again and spoke in a cheerful voice: "I should know her, vrouw," he said, holding the sweet young face between his hands and gazing at it as though he were watching it grow, "I should know her. The same blue eyes, and the lips, and, ah me, the little song she could sing almost before she could stand. But that was long ago," he added with a sigh, looking at her dreamily, "long ago; it's all gone now."

"Not so, indeed," cried Dame Brinker eagerly. "Do you think I would let her forget it? Gretel, child, sing the old song thou hast known so long!"

Raff Brinker's hands fell wearily and his eyes closed, but it was something to see the smile playing about his mouth, as Gretel's voice floated about him like an incense.

It was a simple air; she had never known the words.

With loving instinct she softened every note, until Raff almost fancied that his two-year-old baby was once more beside him.

As soon as the song was finished Hans mounted a wooden stool and began to rummage in the cupboard.

"Have a care, Hans," said Dame Brinker, who through all her poverty was ever a tidy housewife. "Have a care, the wine is there at your right and the white bread beyond it."

"Never fear, mother," answered Hans, reaching far back on an upper shelf, "I shall do no mischief."

Jumping down, he walked toward his father and placed an oblong block of pine-wood in his hands. One of its ends was rounded off and some deep cuts had been made on the top.

"Do you know what it is, father?" asked Hans.

Raff Brinker's face brightened. "Indeed I do, boy; it is the boat I was making for you yest—alack! not yesterday, but years ago."

"I have kept it ever since, father; it can be finished when your hand grows strong again."

"Yes, but not for you, my lad. I must wait for the grandchildren. Why, you are nearly a man. Have you helped your mother, boy, through all these years?"

"Aye, and bravely," put in Dame Brinker.

"Let me see," muttered the father, looking in a puzzled way at them all, "how long is it since the night when the waters were coming in? 'Tis the last I remember."

"We have told thee true, Raff. It was ten years last Pinxter-week."

"Ten years—and I fell then, you say. Has the fever been on me ever since?"

Dame Brinker scarce knew how to reply. Should she tell him all? Tell him that he had been an idiot, almost a lunatic? The doctor had charged her on no account to worry or excite his patient.

Hans and Gretel looked astonished when the answer came.

"Like enough, Raff," she said, nodding her head and raising her eyebrows, "when a heavy man like thee falls on his head it's hard to say what will come—but thou'rt well now, Raff. Thank the good Lord!"

The newly awakened man bowed his head.

"Aye, well enough, mine vrouw," he said, after a moment's

silence, "but my brain turns somehow like a spinning-wheel. It will not be right till I get on the dykes again. When shall I be at work, think you?"

"Hear the man!" cried Dame Brinker, delighted yet frightened, too, for that matter; "we must get him on the bed, Hans. Work indeed!"

They tried to raise him from the chair, but he was not ready yet.

"Be off with ye!" he said, with something like his old smile (Gretel had never seen it before), "does a man want to be lifted about like a log? I tell you before three suns I shall be on the dykes again. Ah! there'll be some stout fellows to greet me. Jan Kamphuisen and young Hoogsvliet. They have been good friends to thee, Hans, I'll warrant."

Hans looked at his mother. Young Hoogsvliet had been dead five years. Jan Kamphuisen was in the jail at Amsterdam.

"Aye, they'd have done their share, no doubt," said Dame Brinker, parrying the inquiry, "had we asked them. But what with working and studying, Hans has been busy enough without seeking comrades."

"Working and studying," echoed Raff, in a musing tone, "can the youngsters read and cipher, Meitje?"

"You should hear them!" she answered proudly. "They can run through a book while I mop the floor. Hans, there, is as happy over a page of big words as a rabbit in a cabbage patch—as for ciphering——"

"Here, lad, help a bit," interrupted Raff Brinker, "I must get me on the bed again."

XXX

THE THOUSAND GUILDERS

NONE seeing the humble supper eaten in the Brinker cottage that night would have dreamed of the dainty fare hidden away near by. Hans and Gretel looked rather wistfully toward the cupboard as they drank their cupful of water and ate their scanty share of black bread, but even in thought they did not rob their father.

"He relished his supper well," said Dame Brinker, nodding sidewise toward the bed, "and fell asleep the next moment—ah, the dear man will be feeble for many a day. He wanted sore to sit up again, but while I made show of humoring him and getting ready, he dropped off. Remember that, my girl, when you have a man of your own (and many a day may it be before that comes to pass), remember, you can never rule by differing; 'humble wife is husband's boss——' Tut! tut! never swallow such a mouthful as that again, child; why, I could make a meal off of two such pieces. What's in thee, Hans? One would think there were cobwebs on the wall."

"Oh, no, mother; I was only thinking——"

"Thinking—about what? Ah, no use asking," she added in a changed tone, "I was thinking of the same a while ago—well, well—it's no blame if we *did* look to hear something by this time about the thousand guilders; but not a word—no—it's plain enough he knows naught about them."

Hans looked up anxiously, dreading lest his mother should grow agitated, as usual, when speaking of the lost money, but she was silently nibbling her bread and looking with a doleful stare toward the window.

"Thousand guilders," echoed a faint voice from the bed. "Ah, I am sure they have been of good use to you, vrouw, through the long years while your man was idle."

The poor woman started up. These words quite destroyed the hope that of late had been glowing within her.

"Are you awake, Raff?" she faltered.

"Yes, Meitje, and I feel much better. Our money was well saved, vrouw, I was saying. Did it last through all those ten years?"

"I—I—have not got it, Raff, I"—she was going to tell him the whole truth, when Hans lifted his finger warningly and whispered:

"Remember what the meester told us; the father must not be worried."

"Speak to him, child," she answered, trembling.

Hans hurried to the bedside.

"I am glad you are feeling better," he said, leaning over his father, "another day will see you quite strong again."

"Aye, like enough. How long did the money last, Hans? I could not hear your mother. What did she say?"

"I said, Raff," stammered Dame Brinker in great distress, "that it was all gone."

"Well, well, wife, do not fret at that; one thousand guilders is not so very much for ten years, and with children to bring up; but it has helped to make you all comfortable. Have you had much sickness to bear?"

"N—no," sobbed Dame Brinker, lifting her apron to her eyes.

THE FROZEN GROUND WAS HARD AS STONE, BUT HANS AND
HIS MOTHER WERE RESOLUTE.

"Tut—tut, woman, why do you cry?" said Raff kindly; "we will soon fill another pouch, when I am on my feet again. Lucky I told you all about it before I fell."

"Told me what, man?"

"Why, that I buried the money. In my dream just now it seemed I had never said aught about it."

Dame Brinker started forward. Hans caught her arm.

"Hist! mother," he whispered, hastily leading her away, "we must be very careful." Then, while she stood with clasped hands waiting in breathless anxiety, he once more approached the cot. Trembling with eagerness he said:

"That was a troublesome dream. Do you remember *when* you buried the money, father?"

"Yes, my boy. It was just before daylight on the same day I was hurt. Jan Kamphuisen said something, the sundown before, that made me distrust his honesty. He was the only one living besides mother who knew we had saved a thousand guilders—so I rose up that night and buried the money—blockhead that I was ever to suspect an old friend!"

"I'll be bound, father," pursued Hans in a laughing voice, motioning to his mother and Gretel to remain quiet—"that you've forgotten where you buried it."

"Ha! ha! not I, indeed—but good-night, my son, I can sleep again."

Hans would have walked away, but his mother's gestures were not to be disobeyed—so he said gently:

"Good-night, father. Where did you say you buried the money? I was only a little one then."

"Close by the willow sapling behind the cottage," said Raff Brinker drowsily.

"Ah, yes. North side of the tree, wasn't it, father?"

"No, the south side. Ah, you know the spot well enough, you rogue—like enough you were there when your mother lifted it. Now, son—easy—shift this pillow—so. Good-night."

"Good-night, father!" said Hans, ready to dance for joy.

The moon rose very late that night, shining in, full and clear, at the little window, but its beams did not disturb Raff Brinker. He slept soundly, so did Gretel. As for Hans and his mother, they had something else to do.

After making a few hurried preparations, they stole forth with bright, expectant faces, bearing a broken spade and a rusty implement that had done many a day's service when Raff was a hale worker on the dykes.

It was so light out of doors they could see the willow tree distinctly. The frozen ground was hard as stone, but Hans and his mother were resolute. Their only dread was that they might disturb the sleepers in the cottage.

"This icebreaker is just the thing, mother," said Hans, striking many a vigorous blow—"but the ground has set so firm it'll be a fair match for it."

"Never fear, Hans," she answered, watching him eagerly, "here, let me try awhile."

They soon succeeded in making an impression; one opening and the rest was not so difficult.

Still they worked on, taking turns and whispering cheerily to one another. Now and then Dame Brinker stepped noiselessly over the threshold and listened, to be certain that her husband slept.

"What grand news it will be for him," she said, laughing, "when he is strong enough to bear it. How I would like to put the pouch and the stocking, just as we find them, all full of money, near him this blessed night, for the dear man to see when he wakens."

"We must get them first, mother," panted Hans, still tugging away at his work.

"There's no doubt of that. They can't slip away from us now," she answered, shivering with cold and excitement, as she crouched beside the opening. "Like enough we'll find them stowed in the old earthen pot I lost long ago."

By this time Hans, too, began to tremble, but not with cold. He had penetrated a foot deep for quite a space on the south side of the tree. At any moment they might come upon the treasure.

"Strange that the dear father should have put it down so woeful deep," said Dame Brinker, in rather a provoked tone. "Ah, the ground was soft enough then, I warrant. How wise of him to mistrust Jan Kamphuisen, and Jan in full credit at the time. Little I thought that handsome fellow with his gay ways would ever go to jail! Now, Hans, let me take a turn—it's lighter work, d'ye see? the deeper we go. I'd be loath to kill the tree, Hans—will we harm it, think you?"

"I cannot say," he answered gravely.

Hour after hour mother and son worked on. The hole grew larger and deeper. Clouds began to gather in the sky, throwing elfish shadows as they passed. Not until moon and stars faded away and streaks of daylight began to appear did Meitje Brinker and Hans look hopelessly into each other's face.

They had searched thoroughly, desperately, all round the tree—south, north, east, west. *The hidden money was not there!*

XXXI

GLIMPSES

ANNIE BOUMAN had a healthy distaste for Janzoon
Kolp. Janzoon Kolp, in his own rough way, adored
Annie. Annie declared she could not, "to save her life," say
one civil word to that odious boy. Janzoon believed her to
be the sweetest, sauciest creature in the world. Annie laughed
among her playmates at the comical flapping of Janzoon's
tattered and dingy jacket; he sighed in solitude over the floating grace of her jaunty blue petticoat. She thanked her stars
that her brothers were not like the Kolps; and he growled
at his sister because she was not like the Boumans. They
seemed to exchange natures whenever they met. His presence
made her harsh and unfeeling, and he, the very sight of *her*
made him gentle as a lamb. Of course they were thrown

together very often. It is thus that in some mysterious way we are convinced of error and cured of prejudice. In this case, however, the scheme failed. Annie detested Janzoon more and more at each encounter, and Janzoon liked her better and better every day.

"He killed a stork, the wicked old wretch!" she would say to herself.

"She knows I am strong and fearless," thought Janzoon.

"How red and freckled and ugly he is!" was Annie's secret comment when she looked at him.

"How she stares and stares!" thought Janzoon. "Well, I am a fine, weatherbeaten fellow, anyway."

"Janzoon Kolp, you impudent boy, go right away from me!" Annie often said, "I don't want any of your company."

"Ha! ha!" laughed Janzoon to himself, "girls never say what they mean. I'll skate with her every chance I can get."

And so it came to pass that the pretty maid would not look up that morning when, skating homeward from Amsterdam, she became convinced that a great, burly boy was coming down the canal toward her.

"Humph! if I look at him," thought Annie, "I'll——"

"Good-morrow, Annie Bouman," said a pleasant voice.

"Good-morrow, Master Hans, I am right glad to meet you."

"Good-morrow, again, Annie. There has been a great change at our house since you left."

"How so?" she exclaimed, opening her eyes very wide.

Hans, who had been in a great hurry and rather moody, grew talkative and quite at leisure in Annie's sunshine. Turning about and skating slowly with her towards Broek, he told the good news of his father. Annie was so true a friend that he told her even of their present distress, of how money was needed, and how everything depended upon his obtaining work, and he could find nothing to do in the neighborhood.

All this was not said as a complaint, but just because she was looking at him, and really wished to know. He could not speak of last night's bitter disappointment, for that secret was not wholly his own.

"Good-bye, Annie!" he said at last. "The morning is going fast and I must haste to Amsterdam and sell these skates. Mother must have money at once. Before nightfall I shall certainly find a job somewhere."

"Sell your new skates, Hans!" cried Annie, "you, the best skater around Broek! Why, the race is coming off in five days."

"I know it," he answered resolutely. "Good-bye! I shall skate home again on the old wooden ones."

Such a bright glance! So different from Janzoon's ugly grin—and Hans was off like an arrow.

"Hans! come back," she called.

Her voice changed the arrow into a top. Spinning around, he darted, in one long, leaning sweep, toward her.

"Then you really are going to sell your new skates if you can find a customer?"

"Of course I am," he replied, looking up with a surprised smile.

"Well, Hans, if you *are* going to sell your skates," said Annie, somewhat confused, "I mean, if you—— Well, I know somebody who would like to buy them—that's all."

"Not Janzoon Kolp?" asked Hans, flushing.

"Oh, no," she pouted, "he is not one of my friends."

"But you *know* him," persisted Hans.

Annie laughed. "Yes, I know him, and it's all the worse for him that I do. Now please, Hans, don't ever talk any more to me about Janzoon. I hate him!"

"Hate him! *you* hate anyone, Annie?"

She shook her head saucily. "Yes; and I'll hate you, too, if you persist in calling him one of my friends. You boys may like him because he caught the greased goose at the Kermis last summer and climbed the pole with his great, ugly body tied up in a sack, but I don't care for such things. I've disliked him ever since I saw him try to push his little sister out of the merry-go-round at Amsterdam; and it's no secret up *our* way who killed the stork on your mother's roof. But we mustn't talk about such a bad, wicked fellow. Really, Hans, I know somebody who would be glad to buy your skates. You won't get half a price for them in Amsterdam. *Please* give them to me. I'll take you the money this very afternoon."

"Annie," he said, taking off the skates and rubbing them carefully with a snarl of twine before handing them to her, "I am sorry to be so particular; but if your friend should not want them, will you bring them back to me today? I must buy peat and meal for the mother early tomorrow morning."

"My friend *will* want them," laughed Annie, nodding gaily, and skating off at the top of her speed.

As Hans drew forth the wooden "runners" from his capacious pockets and fastened them on as best he could, he did not hear Annie murmur, "I wish I had not been so rude; poor, brave Hans; what a noble boy he is!" And as Annie skated homeward filled with pleasant thoughts she did not hear Hans say, "I grumbled like a bear—but, bless her! some girls are like angels!"

Perhaps it was all for the best. One cannot be expected to know everything that is going on in the world.

XXXII

LOOKING FOR WORK

LUXURIES unfit us for returning to hardships easily endured before. The wooden runners squeaked more than ever. It was as much as Hans could do to get on with the clumsy old things; still, he did not regret that he had parted with his beautiful skates—but resolutely pushed back the boyish trouble that he had not been able to keep them just a little longer, at least until after the race.

"Mother surely will not be angry with me," he thought, "for selling them without her leave. She has had care enough already. It will be full time to speak of it when I take home the money."

Hans went up and down the streets of Amsterdam that day, looking for work. He succeeded in earning a few nickels by assisting a man who was driving a train of loaded mules into the city, but he could not secure steady employment anywhere. He would have been glad to obtain a situation as porter or errand boy, but though he passed, on his way, many a loitering, shuffling urchin laden with bundles, there was no place for him. Some shopkeepers had just supplied themselves; others needed a trimmer, more lightly built fellow (they meant better dressed, but did not choose to say so); others told him to call again in a month or two, when the canals would probably be broken up; and many shook their heads at him without saying a word.

At the factories he met with no better luck. It seemed to him that in those great buildings, turning out respectively such tremendous quantities of woolen, cotton and linen stuffs, such world renowned dyes and paints, such precious diamonds cut from the rough, such supplies of meal, of bricks, of glass and china—that in at least one of these a strong-armed boy, able and eager to work, could find something to do. But no—nearly the same answer met him everywhere, "No need of more hands just now."

Toward sundown he returned to Broek, uncertain whether the choking sensation in his throat arose from discouragement or resolution. There was certainly one more chance. Mynheer van Holp might have returned by this time. Master Peter, it was reported, had gone to Haarlem the night before to attend to something connected with the great skating race. Still, Hans would go and try.

Fortunately Peter had returned early that morning. He was at home when Hans reached there and was just about starting for the Brinker cottage.

"Ah, Hans!" he cried, as the weary boy approached the door. "You are the very one I wished to see. Come in and warm yourself."

After tugging at his well-worn hat, which always *would* stick to his head when he was embarrassed, Hans knelt down— not by way of making a new style of Oriental salute—nor to worship the goddess of cleanliness who presided there—but because his heavy shoes would have filled the soul of a Broek housewife with horror. When their owner stepped softly into the house they were left outside to act as sentinels until his return.

Hans left the Van Holp mansion with a lightened heart. Peter had brought word from Haarlem that young Brinker was to commence working upon the summer-house doors immediately. There was a comfortable workshop on the place and it was to be at his service until the carving was done.

Peter did not tell Hans that he had skated all the way to Haarlem for the purpose of arranging this plan with Mynheer van Holp. It was enough for him to see the glad, eager look rise on young Brinker's face.

"I *think* I can do it," said Hans, "though I have never learned the trade."

"I am *sure* you can," responded Peter heartily. "You will find every tool you require in the workshop. It is nearly hidden yonder by that wall of twigs. In summer, when the hedge is green, one cannot see the shop from here at all. How is your father today?"

"Better, mynheer—he improves every hour."

"It is the most astonishing thing I ever heard of. That gruff old doctor is a great fellow after all."

"Ah! mynheer," said Hans warmly, "he is more than great. He is good. But for the meester's kind heart and great skill my poor father would yet be in the dark. I think, mynheer," he added, with kindling eyes, "surgery is the very noblest science in the world!"

Peter shrugged his shoulders. "Very noble it may be, but not quite to my taste. This Doctor Boekman certainly has skill. As for his heart—defend me from such hearts as his!"

"Why do you say so, mynheer?" asked Hans.

Just then a lady slowly entered from an adjoining apartment. It was Mevrouw van Holp arrayed in the grandest of caps and the longest of satin aprons ruffled with lace. She nodded placidly as Hans stepped back from the fire, bowing as well as he knew how.

Peter at once drew a high-backed oaken chair toward the fire and the lady seated herself. There was a block of cork on each side of the chimney-place. One of these he placed under his mother's feet.

Hans turned to go.

"Wait a moment, if you please, young man," said the lady. "I accidentally overheard you and my son speaking, I think, of my friend Doctor Boekman. You are right, young man. Doctor Boekman has a very kind heart. You perceive, Peter, we may be quite mistaken in judging of persons solely by their manners, though a courteous deportment is by no means to be despised."

"I intended no disrespect, mother," said Peter, "but surely one has no right to go growling and snarling through the world, as they say he does."

" 'They say.' Ah, Peter, 'they' means everybody or nobody. Surgeon Boekman has had a great sorrow. Many years ago he lost his only child, under very painful circumstances—a fine lad, except that he was a thought too hasty and high-spirited. Before then, Gerard Boekman was one of the most agreeable gentlemen I ever knew."

So saying, Mevrouw van Holp, looking kindly upon the two boys, arose and left the room with the same dignity with which she had entered.

Peter, only half convinced, muttered something about "the sin of allowing sorrow to turn all one's honey into gall," as he conducted his visitor to the narrow side-door. Before they parted he advised Hans to keep himself in good skating order, "for," he added, "now that your father is all right, you will be in fine spirits for the race. That will be the prettiest skating show ever seen in this part of the world. Everybody is talking of it. You are to try for the prize, remember."

"I shall not be in the race, mynheer," said Hans, looking down.

"Not be in the race! Why not indeed?" and immediately Peter's thoughts swept on a full tide of suspicion towards Carl Schummel.

"Because I cannot, mynheer," answered Hans, as he bent to slip his feet into his big shoes.

Something in the boy's manner warned Peter that it would be no kindness to press the matter further. He bade Hans "Good-bye" and stood thoughtfully watching him as he walked away.

In a minute Peter called out:

"Hans Brinker!"

"Yes, mynheer."

"I'll take back all I said about Doctor Boekman."

"Yes, mynheer."

Both were laughing, but Peter's smile changed to a look of puzzled surprise when he saw Hans kneel down by the canal and put on the wooden skates.

"Very queer," muttered Peter, shaking his head as he turned to go into the house, "why in the world don't the boy wear his new ones?"

XXXIII

THE FAIRY GODMOTHER

THE sun had gone down quite out of sight when our hero—
with a happy heart but with something like a sneer on
his countenance as he jerked off the wooden "runners"—
trudged hopefully toward the tiny, hut-like building known
of old as the Idiot's Cottage.

Duller eyes than his would have discerned two slight fig-
ures moving near the doorway.

That gray, well-patched jacket and the dull blue skirt
covered with an apron of still duller blue, that faded, close-
fitting cap, and those quick little feet in their great boat-like
shoes,—they were Gretel's, of course. He would have known
them anywhere.

That bright, coquettish red jacket, with its pretty skirt

186

bordered with black, that graceful cap bobbing over the gold ear-rings, that dainty apron, and those snug leather shoes that seemed to have grown with the feet—why, if the Pope of Rome had sent them to him by express, Hans could have sworn they were Annie's.

The two girls were slowly pacing up and down in front of the cottage. Their arms were entwined, of course, and their heads were nodding and shaking as emphatically as if all the affairs of the kingdom were under discussion.

With a joyous shout Hans hastened toward them.

"Huzza, girls, I've found work!"

This brought his mother to the cottage-door.

She, too, had pleasant tidings. The father was still improving. He had been sitting up nearly all day, and was now sleeping, as Dame Brinker declared, "just as quiet as a lamb."

"It is my turn now, Hans," said Annie, drawing him aside after he had told his mother the good word from Mynheer van Holp. "Your skates are sold and here's the money."

"Seven guilders!" cried Hans, counting the pieces in astonishment; "why, that is three times as much as I paid for them."

"I cannot help that," said Annie. "If the buyer knew no better, it is not our fault."

Hans looked up quickly.

"Oh, Annie!"

"Oh, Hans!" she mimicked, pursing her lips and trying to look desperately wicked and unprincipled.

"Now, Annie, I know you would never mean that! You must return some of this money."

"But I'll not do any such thing," insisted Annie, "they're sold, and that's an end of it." Then, seeing that he looked really pained, she added in a lower tone:

"Will you believe me, Hans, when I say that there has been no mistake—that the person who bought your skates *insisted* upon paying seven guilders for them?"

"I will," he answered—and the light from his clear blue eyes seemed to settle and sparkle under Annie's lashes.

Dame Brinker was delighted at the sight of so much silver, but when she learned that Hans had parted with his treasures to obtain it, she sighed, as she exclaimed:

"Bless thee, child! That will be a sore loss for thee!"

"Here, mother," said the boy, plunging his hand far into his pocket, "here is more—we shall be rich if we keep on!"

"Aye, indeed," she answered, eagerly reaching forth her hand. Then, lowering her voice, added, "We *would* be rich but for that Jan Kamphuisen. He was at the willow tree years ago, Hans—depend upon it!"

"Indeed, it seems likely," sighed Hans; "well, mother, we must give up the money bravely. It is certainly gone—the father has told us all he knows. Let us think no more about it."

"That's easy saying, Hans. I shall try, but it's hard, and my poor man wanting so many comforts. Bless me! how girls fly about. They were here but this instant. Where did they run to?"

"They slipped behind the cottage," said Hans, "like enough to hide from us. Hist! I'll catch them for you! They both can move quicker and softer than yonder rabbit, but I'll give them a good star first."

"Why, there *is* a rabbit, sure enough. Hold! Hans, the poor thing must have been in sore need to venture from its burrow this bitter weather. I'll get a few crumbs for it within."

So saying, the good woman bustled into the cottage. She

soon came out again, but Hans had forgotten to wait and the rabbit, after taking a cool survey of the premises, had scampered off to unknown quarters. Turning the corner of the cottage, Dame Brinker came upon the children. Hans and Gretel were standing before Annie, who was seated carelessly upon a stump.

"That is as good as a picture!" cried Dame Brinker, halting in admiration of the group. "Many a painting have I seen at the grand house at Heidelberg not a whit prettier. My two are rough chubs, ·Annie, but *you* look like a fairy."

"Do I?" laughed Annie, sparkling with animation. "Well, then, Gretel and Hans, imagine I'm your godmother just paying you a visit. Now I'll grant you each a wish. What will you have, Master Hans?"

A shade of earnestness passed over Annie's face as she looked up at him—perhaps it was because she wished from the depths of her heart that for once she could have a fairy's power.

Something whispered to Hans that, for the moment, she was more than mortal.

"I wish," said he, solemnly, "I could find something I was searching for last night."

Gretel laughed merrily. Dame Brinker moaned "Shame on you, Hans!" and passed wearily into the cottage.

The fairy godmother sprang up and stamped her foot three times.

"Thou shalt have thy wish," said she, "let them say what they will." Then, with playful solemnity, she put her hand into her apron pocket and drew forth a large glass bead. "Bury this," said she, giving it to Hans, "where I have stamped and ere moonrise thy wish shall be granted."

Gretel laughed more merrily than ever.

The godmother pretended great displeasure.

"Naughty child," said she, scowling terribly. "In punishment for laughing at a fairy, *thy* wish shall not be granted."

"Ha!" cried Gretel in high glee, "better wait till you're asked, godmother. I haven't made any wish!"

Annie acted her part well. Never smiling through all their merry laughter, she stalked away, the embodiment of offended dignity.

"Good-night, fairy!" they cried again and again.

"Good-night, mortals!" she called out at last, as she sprang over a frozen ditch and ran toward her home.

"Oh, isn't she—just like flowers—so sweet and lovely!" cried Gretel, looking after her in great admiration, "and to think how many days she stays in that dark room with her grandmother. Why, brother Hans! What is the matter? What are you going to do?"

"Wait and see!" answered Hans, as he plunged into the cottage and came out again, all in an instant, bearing the spade and icebreaker in his hands—"I'm going to bury my magic bead!"

Raff Brinker still slept soundly; his wife took a small block of peat from her nearly exhausted store and put it upon the embers. Then, opening the door, she called gently:

"Come in, children."

"Mother! mother! See here!" shouted Hans.

"Holy Saint Bavon!" exclaimed the dame, springing over the doorstep. "What ails the boy!"

"Come quick, mother," he cried, in great excitement, working with all his might and driving in the icebreaker at each word. "Don't you see? *This* is the spot—right here on the south side of the stump. Why didn't we think of it last night?

The *stump* is the old willow tree—the one you cut down last spring because it shaded the potatoes. That little tree wasn't here when father—Huzza!"

Dame Brinker could not speak. She dropped on her knees beside Hans just in time to see him drag forth—*the old stone pot!*

He thrust in his hand and took out—a piece of brick—then another—then another—then the stocking and the pouch, black and moldy, but filled with the long lost treasure!

Such a time! Such laughing! Such crying! Such counting, after they went into the cottage! It was a wonder that Raff did not waken. His dreams were pleasant, however, for he smiled in his sleep.

Dame Brinker and her children had a fine supper I can assure you. No need of saving the delicacies now.

"We'll get father some nice fresh things tomorrow," said the dame, as she brought forth cold meat, wine, bread and jelly, and placed them on the clean pine table. "Sit by, children, sit by."

———

That night Annie fell asleep wondering whether it was a knife Hans had lost, and thinking how funny it would be if he should find it, after all.

Hans had scarce closed his eyes before he found himself trudging through a thicket; pots of gold were lying all around, and watches, and skates, and glittering beads were swinging from every branch.

Strange to say, each tree, as he approached it, changed into a stump, and on the stump sat the prettiest fairy imaginable, clad in a scarlet jacket and blue petticoat.

XXXIV

THE MYSTERIOUS WATCH

SOMETHING else than the missing guilders was brought to light on the day of the fairy godmother's visit. This was the story of the watch that for ten long years had been so jealously guarded by Raff's faithful vrouw. Through many an hour of sore temptation she had dreaded almost to look upon it, lest she might be tempted to disobey her husband's request. It had been hard to see her children hungry and to know that the watch, if sold, would enable the roses to bloom in their cheeks again—"but nay," she would exclaim, "Meitje Brinker is not one to forget her man's last bidding, come what may."

"Take good care of this, mine vrouw," he had said, as he handed it to her ten years ago. No explanation followed, for the words were scarcely spoken, when one of his fellow workmen rushed into the cottage, crying, "Come, man! the waters are rising! You're wanted on the dykes."

Raff had started at once and that, as Dame Brinker has already told you, was the last she saw of him in his right mind.

On the day when Hans was in Amsterdam looking for work, and Gretel, after performing her household labors, was wandering about in search of chips, twigs—anything that could be burned, Dame Brinker with suppressed excitement had laid the watch in her husband's hand.

"It wasn't in reason," as she afterwards said to Hans, "to wait any longer, when a word from the father would settle all; no woman living but would want to know how he came by that watch."

Raff Brinker turned the bright, polished thing over and over in his hand—then he examined the bit of smoothly ironed black ribbon fastened to it; he seemed hardly to recognize it. At last he said, "Ah, I remember this! Why, you've been rubbing it, vrouw, till it shines like a new guilder."

"Aye," said Dame Brinker, nodding her head complacently.

Raff looked at it again. "Poor boy!" he murmured, then fell into a brown study.

"Is the man—the lad—thou wert talking of dead, think thee?" asked the vrouw, hiding the watch in her hand, but seating herself expectantly on the end of his long foot-bench.

"It's hard telling," he answered.

"Was he so sick, Raff?"

"No, not sick, I may say; but troubled, vrouw, very troubled."

"Had he done any wrong, think ye?" she asked, lowering her voice.

Raff nodded.

"*Murder?*" whispered the wife, not daring to look up.

"He said it was like to that, indeed."

"Oh Raff, you frighten me—tell me more—you speak so strangely—and you tremble. I must know all."

"If I tremble, mine vrouw, it must be from the fever. There is no guilt on my soul, thank God!"

"Take a sip of this wine, Raff. There, now you are better. It was like to a crime, you were saying."

"Aye, Meitje, like to murder; *that* he told me himself.

But I'll never believe it. A likely lad, fresh and honest-look-
ing as our own youngster, but with something not so bold
and straight about him."

"Aye, I know," said the dame gently, fearing to inter-
rupt the story.

"He came upon me quite sudden," continued Raff. "I
had never seen his face before—the palest, frightenedest face
that ever was. He caught me by the arm—'You look like
an honest man,' says he."

"Aye, he was right in that," interrupted the dame, emphatically.

Raff looked somewhat bewildered.

"Where was I, mine vrouw?"

"The lad took hold of your arm, Raff," she said, gazing
at him anxiously.

"Aye, so. The words come awkward to me and everything is half like a dream, ye see."

"S-stut! What wonder, poor man," sighed the dame,
stroking his hand. "If ye had not head enough for a dozen,
the wit would never have come to ye again. Well, the lad
caught ye by the arm and said ye looked honest (well he
might!) What then? Was it noon-time?"

"Nay; before daylight—long before early chimes."

"It was the same day you were hurt," said the dame.
"I know it seemed you went to your work in the middle of
the night. You left off where he caught your arm, Raff."

"Yes," resumed her husband—"and I can see his face
this minute—so white and wild-looking. 'Take me down the
river a way,' says he. I was working then, you'll remember,
far down the line, across from Amsterdam. I told him I was
no boatman. 'It's an affair of life and death,' says he,

'take me on a few miles—yonder skiff is not locked, but it
may be a poor man's boat and I'd be loath to rob him!' (The
words might differ some, vrouw, for it's all like a dream.)
Well, I took him down; it might be six or eight miles, and
then he said he could run the rest of the way on shore. I
was in haste to get the boat back. Before he jumped out,
he says, sobbing-like, 'I can trust you. I've done a thing—
God knows I never intended it—but the man is dead. I must
fly from Holland.' "

"What was it, did he say, Raff? Had he been shooting
at a comrad, like they do down at the University at Got-
tingen?"

"I can't recall that. Mayhap he told me; but it's all
like a dream. I said it wasn't for me, a good Hollander, to
cheat the laws of my country by helping him off that way;
but he kept saying, 'God knows I am innocent!' and looked
at me in the starlight as fair, now, and clear-eyed as our little
Hans might—and I just pulled away faster.

"Well, just before jumping from the boat he says, handing me the watch, 'I'm flying from my country, as I never
thought I could. I'll trust you because you look honest. Will
you take this to my father—not today but in a week, and tell
him his unhappy boy sent it; and tell him if ever the time
comes that he wants me to come back to him, I'll brave everything and come. Tell him to send a letter to—to'—there, the
rest is all gone from me. I *can't* remember where the letter
was to go. Poor lad! poor lad," resumed Raff, sorrowfully,
taking the watch from his vrouw's lap as he spoke—"and it's
never been sent to his father to this day."

"I'll take it, Raff, never fear—the moment Gretel gets
back. She will be in soon. What was the father's name,
did you say? Where were you to find him?"

"Alack!" answered Raff, speaking very slowly, "It's all slipped me. I can see the lad's face, and his great eyes, just as plain—and I remember his opening the watch and snatching something from it and kissing it—but no more. All the rest whirls past me; there's a kind of sound like rushing waters comes over me when I try to think."

"Aye. That's plain to see, Raff; but I've had the same feeling after a fever. You're tired now—I must get ye straight on the bed again. Where *is* the child, I wonder?"

Dame Brinker opened the door and called "Gretel! Gretel!"

"Stand aside, vrouw," said Raff feebly, as he leaned forward and endeavored to look out upon the bare landscape, "I've half a mind to stand beyond the door just once."

"Nay, nay," she laughed, "I'll tell the meester how ye tease, and fidget, and bother to be let out in the air; and, if he says it, I'll bundle ye warm tomorrow and give ye a turn on your feet. But I'm freezing you with this door open. I declare, if there isn't Gretel with her apron full, skating on the canal like wild. Why, man," she continued, almost in a scream, as she slammed the door, "thou'rt walking to the bed without my touching thee! Thou'lt fall!"

The dame's "thee" proved her mingled fear and delight even more than the rush which she made toward her husband. Soon he was comfortably settled under the new cover, declaring, as his vrouw tucked him in snugly and warmly, that it was the last daylight that should see him abed.

"Aye! I can hope it myself," laughed Dame Brinker, "now you have been frisking about at that rate." As Raff closed his eyes the dame hastened to revive her fire, or rather to dull it, for Dutch peat is like a Dutchman, slow to kindle, but very good at a blaze when once started. Then, putting her neglected spinning-wheel away, she drew forth her knitting from some invisible pocket and seated herself by the bedside.

"If you could remember that man's name, Raff," she began cautiously, "I might take the watch to him while you're sleeping; Gretel can't but be in soon."

Raff tried to think, but in vain.

"Could it be Boomphoffen?" suggested the dame. "I've heard how they've had two sons turn out bad—Gerard and Lambert."

"It might be," said Raff. "Look if there's letters on the watch, that'll guide us some."

"Bless thee, man," cried the happy dame, eagerly lifting the watch, "why, thou'rt sharper than ever! Sure enough. Here's letters! L. J. B. That's Lambert Boomphoffen, you may depend; what the J is for I can't say; but they used to be grand kind o' people, high-feathered as fancy fowl. Just the kind to give their children all double names, which isn't Scripture anyway."

"I don't know about that, vrouw. Seems to me there's long mixed names in the Holy Book, hard enough to make out. But you've got the right guess at a jump. It was your way always," said Raff, closing his eyes. "Take the watch to Boompkinks and try."

"Not Boompkinks, I know no such name; it's Boomphoffen."

"Aye, take it there."

"Take it there, man! Why, the whole brood of 'em's been gone to America these four years. But go to sleep, Raff; you look pale and out of strength. It'll come to you, what's best to do, in the morning."

"So, Mistress Gretel! Here you are at last!"

Before Raff awoke that evening the fairy godmother, as we know, had been at the cottage, the guilders were once more safely locked in the big chest, and Dame Brinker and the children were faring sumptuously on meat and white bread and wine.

So the mother, in the joy of her heart, told them the story of the watch as far as she deemed it prudent to divulge it. It was no more than fair, she thought, that the poor things should know, after keeping the secret so safe, ever since they had been old enough to know anything.

XXXV

A DISCOVERY

THE next sun brought a busy day to the Brinkers.

In the first place, the news of the thousand guilders had, of course, to be told to the father. Such tidings as that surely could not harm him.

After dinner the affair of the watch was talked over and the mysterious initials duly discussed.

Hans had just pushed back his stool, intending to start at once for Mynheer van Holp's, and his mother had risen to put the watch away in its old hiding-place, when they heard the sound of wheels upon the frozen ground.

Someone knocked at the door, opening it at the same time.

"Come in," stammered Dame Brinker, hastily trying to hide the watch in her bosom. "Oh! is it you, mynheer! Good-day, the father is nearly well, as you see. It's a poor place to greet you in, mynheer, and the dinner not cleared away."

Doctor Boekman scarcely noticed the dame's apology. He was evidently in haste.

"Ahem!" he exclaimed, "not needed here, I perceive. The patient is mending fast."

"Well he may, mynheer," cried the dame, "for only last night we found a thousand guilders that's been lost to us these ten years."

Doctor Boekman opened his eyes.

"Yes, mynheer," said Raff. "I bid the vrouw tell you, though it's to be held a secret among us, for I see you can keep your lips closed as well as any man."

The doctor scowled. He never liked personal remarks.

"Now, mynheer," continued Raff, "you can take your rightful pay. God knows you have earned it, if bringing such a poor tool back to the world and his family can be called a service. Tell the vrouw what's to pay, mynheer; she will hand out the sum right willingly."

"Tut! tut!" said the doctor kindly. "Say nothing about money. I can find plenty of such pay any time, but gratitude comes seldom. That boy's 'Thank you,' " he added, nodding sidewise towards Hans, "was pay enough for me."

"Like enough ye have a boy of your own," said Dame Brinker, quite delighted to see the great man becoming so sociable.

Doctor Boekman's good-nature vanished at once. He gave a growl (at least, it seemed so to Gretel), but made no actual reply.

"Do not think the vrouw meddlesome, mynheer," said Raff, "she has been sore touched of late about a lad whose folks have gone away, none know where, and I had a message for them from the young gentleman."

"The name was Boomphoffen," said the dame eagerly. "Do you know aught of the family, mynheer?"

The doctor's reply was brief and gruff.

"Yes. A troublesome set. They went long since to America."

"It might be, Raff," persisted Dame Brinker, timidly, "that the meester knows somebody in that country, though I'm told they are mostly savages over there. If he could get the watch to the Boomphoffens with the poor lad's message, it would be a most blessed thing."

"Tut! vrouw, why pester the good meester and dying men and women wanting him everywhere. How do ye know ye have the true name?"

"I'm sure of it," she replied. "They had a son Lambert, and there's an L for Lambert, and a B for Boomphoffen, on the back; though, to be sure, there's an odd J, too; but the meester can look for himself."

So saying, she drew forth the watch.

"L. J. B.!" cried Doctor Boekman, springing toward her.

Why attempt to describe the scene that followed! I need only say that the lad's message was delivered to his father at last—delivered while the great surgeon was sobbing like a little child.

"Laurens! my Laurens!" he cried, gazing with yearning eyes at the watch as he held it tenderly in his palm. "Ah, if I had but known sooner! Laurens a homeless wanderer— Great Heaven! he may be suffering, dying at this moment! Think, man, where is he? Where did my boy say the letter must be sent?"

Raff shook his head sadly.

"Think!" implored the doctor. Surely the memory so lately awakened through his aid could not refuse to serve him in a moment like this.

"'It is all gone, mynheer," sighed Raff.

Hans, forgetting distinctions of rank and station, forgetting everything but that his good friend was in trouble, threw his arms around the doctor's neck.

"I can find your son, mynheer. If alive, he is *somewhere*. The earth is not so very large; I will devote every day of my life to the search. Mother can spare me now. You are rich, mynheer; send me where you will."

Gretel began to cry. It was right for Hans to go, but how could they ever live without him?

Doctor Boekman made no reply, neither did he push Hans away. His eyes were fixed anxiously upon Raff Brinker. Suddenly he lifted the watch and with trembling eagerness attempted to open it. Its stiffened spring yielded at last; the case flew open, disclosing a watch-paper in the back bearing a group of blue forget-me-nots. Raff, seeing a shade of intense disappointment pass over the doctor's face, hastened to say:

"There was something else in it, mynheer, but the young gentleman tore it out before he handed it to me. I saw him kiss it as he put it away."

"It was his mother's picture," moaned the doctor, "she died when he was ten years old. Thank God! the boy had not forgotten. Both dead? It is impossible!" he cried, starting up. "My boy is alive. You shall hear his story. Laurens acted as my assistant. By mistake he portioned out the wrong medicine for one of my patients—a deadly poison—but it was never administered, for I discovered the error in time. The man died that day. I was detained with other bad cases until the next evening. When I reached home my boy was gone. Poor Laurens!" sobbed the doctor, breaking down completely, "never to hear from me through all these years—his message disregarded. Oh, what must he have suffered!"

Dame Brinker ventured to speak. Anything was better than to see the meester cry.

"It is a mercy to know the young gentleman was innocent. Ah! how he fretted! Telling you, Raff, that his crime was like unto murder. It was sending the wrong physic he meant. Crime indeed! Why, our own Gretel might have done that! Like enough the poor young gentleman heard that the man was dead—that's why he ran, mynheer. He said, you know, Raff, that he never could come back to Holland again, unless"—she hesitated—"ah, your honor, ten years is a dreary time to be waiting to hear from——"

"Hist, vrouw!" said Raff sharply.

"Waiting to hear," groaned the doctor, "and I, like a fool sitting stubbornly at home, thinking he had abandoned me. I never dreamed, Brinker, that the boy had discovered the mistake. I believed it was youthful folly—ingratitude—love of adventure, that sent him away. My poor, poor Laurens!"

"But you know all now, mynheer," whispered Hans. "You know he was innocent of wrong, that he loved you and his dead mother. We will find him. You shall see him again, dear meester."

"God bless you!" said Dr. Boekman, seizing the boy's hand, "it may be as you say. I shall try—I shall try—and, Brinker, if ever the faintest gleam of recollection concerning him should come to you, you will send me word at once?"

"Indeed we will!" cried all but Hans, whose silent promise would have satisfied the doctor even had the others not spoken.

"Your boy's eyes," he said, turning to Dame Brinker, "are strangely like my son's. The first time I met him it seemed that Laurens himself was looking at me."

"Aye, mynheer," replied the mother proudly. "I have marked that you were much drawn to the child."

For a few moments the meester seemed lost in thought; then, rousing himself, he spoke in a new voice:

"Forgive me, Raff Brinker, for this tumult. Do not feel distressed on my account. I leave your house today a happier man than I have been for many a long year. Shall I take the watch?"

"Certainly you must, mynheer. It was your son's wish."

"Even so," responded the doctor, regarding his treasure with a queer frown, for his face could not throw off its bad habits in an hour—"even so. And now I must be gone. No medicine is needed by my patient; only peace and cheerfulness, and both are here in plenty. Heaven bless you, my good friends! I shall ever be grateful to you."

"May Heaven bless you, too, mynheer, and may you soon find the dear young gentleman," said Dame Brinker earnestly, after hurriedly wiping her eyes upon the corner of her apron.

Raff uttered a hearty "Amen!" and Gretel threw such a wistful, eager glance at the doctor that he patted her head as he turned to leave the cottage.

Hans went out also.

"When I can serve you, mynheer, I am ready."

"Very well, boy," replied Doctor Boekman with peculiar mildness. "Tell them within to say nothing of what has just passed. Meantime, Hans, when you are with your father, watch his mood. You have tact. At any moment he may suddenly be able to tell us more."

"Trust me for that, mynheer."

"Good-day, my boy!" cried the doctor, as he sprang into his stately coach.

"Aha!" thought Hans, as it rolled away, "the meester has more life in him than I thought."

XXXVI

THE RACE

THE twentieth of December came at last, bringing with it the perfection of winter weather. All over the level landscape lay the warm sunlight.

There was an end to grinding, crushing and sawing for that day. It was a good thing for the millers near Broek. Long before noon they concluded to take in their sails and go to the race. Everybody would be there—already the north side of the frozen Y was bordered with eager spectators; the news of the great skating match had traveled far and wide. Men, women and children in holiday attire were flocking toward the spot. Some wore furs, and wintry cloaks or shawls; but many, consulting their feelings rather than the almanac, were dressed as for an October day.

The site selected for the race was a faultless plain of ice near Amsterdam, on the great *arm* of the Zuyder-Zee, which Dutchmen, of course, must call—the *Eye*. The towns-people turned out in large numbers. Strangers in the city deemed it a fine chance to see what was to be seen.

There seemed to be at least one specimen from every known town in Holland. There were Utrecht water-bearers, Gouda cheese-makers, Delft potterymen, Schiedam distillers, Amsterdam diamond-cutters, Rotterdam merchants, dried-up herring-packers, and two sleepy-eyed shepherds from Texel. Every man of them had his pipe and tobacco pouch.

You know quite a number among the spectators. High up in yonder pavilion, erected upon the border of the ice, are some persons whom you have seen very lately. In the center is Madame van Gleck. It is her birthday, you remem-ber; she has the post of honor. There is Mynheer van Gleck, whose meerschaum has not really grown fast to his lips—it only appears so. There are grandfather and grandmother, whom you met at the Saint Nicholas fete. All the children are with them. It is so mild they have brought even the baby. The poor little creature is swaddled very much after the man-ner of an Egyptian mummy, but it can crow with delight and, when the band is playing, open and shut its animated mittens in perfect time to the music.

Grandfather, with his pipe and spectacles and fur cap, makes quite a picture as he holds baby upon his knee. Perched high upon their canopied platform the party can see all that is going on. No wonder the ladies look complacently at the glassy ice; with a stove for a foot-stool one might sit cozily beside the North Pole.

There is a gentleman with them who somewhat resembles Saint Nicholas as he appeared to the Young Van Glecks, on the fifth of December. But the saint had a flowing white beard, and this face is as smooth as a pippin. His saintship was larger around the body, too, and (between ourselves) he had a pair of thimbles in his mouth, which this gentleman certainly has not. It cannot be Saint Nicholas after all.

Near by, in the next pavilion, sit the Van Holps with their son and daughter (the Van Gends), from The Hague. Peter's sister is not one to forget her promises. She has brought bouquets of exquisite hot-house flowers for the winners.

These pavilions, and there are others besides, have all been erected since daylight. That semi-circular one, containing Mynheer van Korbes' family, is very pretty and proves that the Hollanders are quite skilled at tent-making, but I like the Van Glecks' best—the center one—striped red and white, and hung with evergreens.

The one with the blue flags contains the musicians. Those pagoda-like affairs, decked with sea-shells and streamers of every possible hue, are the judges' stands; and those columns and flagstaffs upon the ice mark the limit of the race-course. The two white columns twined with green, connected at the top by that long, floating strip of drapery, form the starting-point. Those flag-staffs, half a mile off, stand at each end of the boundary line, cut sufficiently deep to be distinct to the skaters, though not enough so as to trip them when they turn to come back to the starting-point.

Holland is the place for skaters after all. Where else can nearly every boy and girl perform feats on the ice that would attract a crowd if seen in Central Park? Look at Ben! I did not see him before. He is really astonishing the natives, no easy thing to do in the Netherlands. Save your strength, Ben, you will need it soon. Now other boys are trying! Ben is surpassed already. Such jumping, such poising, such spinning, such india-rubber exploits generally!

There are some familiar faces near the white columns. Lambert, Ludwig, Peter and Carl are all there, cool and in good skating order. Hans is not far off. Evidently he is going to join in the race, for his skates are on—the very pair that he sold for seven guilders! He had soon suspected that his fairy godmother was the mysterious "friend" who bought them. This settled, he had boldly charged her with the deed, and she, knowing well that all her little savings had been spent in the purchase, had not had the face to deny it. Through the fairy godmother, too, he had been rendered amply able to buy them back again. Therefore Hans is to be in the race. Carl is more indignant than ever about it, but as three other peasant boys have entered, Hans is not alone.

Twenty boys and twenty girls. The latter by this time are standing in front, braced for the start, for they are to have the first "run." Hilda, Rychie and Katrinka are among them—two or three bend hastily to give a last pull at their skate-straps. It is pretty to see them stamp, to be sure that all is firm. Hilda is speaking pleasantly to a graceful little creature in a red jacket and a new brown petticoat. Why, it is Gretel! What a difference those pretty shoes make, and the skirt, and the new cap. Even Janzoon Kolp's sister has been admitted—but Janzoon himself has been voted out by the directors, because he killed the stork and only last summer was caught in the act of robbing a bird's nest, a legal offense in Holland.

Twenty girls are formed in a line. The music has ceased.

A man, whom we shall call The Crier, stands between the columns and the first judges' stand. He reads the rules in a loud voice:

"The girls and boys are to race in turn, until one girl and one boy has beaten twice. They are to start in a line from the united columns—skate to the flag-staff line, turn and then come back to the starting-point, thus making a mile at each run."

A flag is waved from the judges' stand. Madame van Gleck rises in her pavilion. She leans forward with a white handkerchief in her hand. When she drops it a bugler is to give the signal for them to start.

The handkerchief is fluttering to the ground. Hark!

They are off!

No. Back again. Their line was not true in passing the judges' stand.

The signal is repeated.

Off again. No mistake this time. Whew! how fast they go!

The multitude is quiet for an instant, absorbed in eager, breathless watching.

Cheers spring up along the line of spectators. Huzza! five girls are ahead. Who comes flying back from the boundary mark? We cannot tell. Something red, that is all. There is a blue spot flitting near it and a dash of yellow nearer still. Spectators at this end of the line strain their eyes and wish they had taken their post nearer the flag-staff.

The wave of cheers is coming back again. Now we can see! Katrinka is ahead!

She passes the Van Holp pavilion. The next is Madame van Gleck's. That leaning figure gazing from it is a magnet. Hilda shoots past Katrinka, waving her hand to her mother as she passes. Two others are close now, whizzing on like arrows. What is that flash of red and gray? Hurrah, it is Gretel! She, too, waves her hand, but toward no gay pavilion.

The crowd is cheering, but she hears only her father's voice, "Well done, little Gretel!" Soon Katrinka, with a quick, merry laugh, shoots past Hilda. The girl in yellow is gaining now. She passes them all, all except Gretel. The judges lean forward without seeming to lift their eyes from their watches. Cheer after cheer fills the air; the very columns seem rocking. Gretel has passed them. She has won.

"Gretel Brinker—one mile!" shouts The Crier.

The judges nod. They write something upon a tablet which each holds in his hand.

While the girls are resting—some crowding eagerly around our frightened little Gretel, some standing aside in high disdain—the boys form in a line.

Mynheer van Gleck drops the handkerchief this time. The buglers give a vigorous blast!

The boys have started.

Half-way already! Did ever you see the like!

Three hundred legs flashing by in an instant. But there are only twenty boys. No matter, there were hundreds of legs, I am sure! Where are they now? There is such a noise one gets bewildered. What are the people laughing at? Oh, at that fat boy in the rear. See him go! See him! He'll be down in an instant—no, he won't. I wonder if he knows he is all alone; the other boys are nearly at the boundary line. Yes, he knows it. He stops! He wipes his hot face. He takes off his cap and looks about him. Better to give up with good grace. He has made a hundred friends by that hearty, astonished laugh. Good Jacob Poot!

The fine fellow is already among the spectators gazing as eagerly as the rest.

A cloud of feathery ice flies from the heels of the skaters as they "bring to" and turn at the flag-staffs.

Something black is coming now, one of the boys—it is all we know. Now they come nearer—we can see the red cap. There's Ben—there's Peter—there's Hans!

Hans is ahead! Young Madame van Gend almost crushes the flowers in her hand; she had been quite sure that Peter would be first. Carl Schummel is next, then Ben, and the youth with the red cap. The others are pressing close. A tall figure darts among them. He passes the red cap, he passes Ben, then Carl. Now it is an even race between him and Hans. Madame van Gend catches her breath.

It is Peter! He is ahead! Hans shoots past him. Hilda's eyes fill with tears, Peter *must* beat. Annie's eyes flash proudly. Gretel gazes with clasped hands—four strokes more will take her brother to the columns.

He is there! Yes, but so was young Schummel just a second before. At the last instant Carl, gathering his powers, had whizzed between them and passed the goal.

"Carl Schummel—one mile!" shouts The Crier.

Soon Madame van Gleck rises again. The falling handkerchief starts the bugle, and the bugle, using its voice as a bow-string, shoots off twenty girls like so many arrows.

It is a beautiful sight, but one has not long to look; before we can fairly distinguish them they are far in the distance. This time they are close upon one another; it is hard to say as they come speeding back from the flag-staff which will reach the columns first. There are new faces among the foremost—eager, glowing faces, unnoticed before. Katrinka is there, and Hilda; but Gretel and Rychie are in the rear. Gretel is wavering, but when Rychie passes her, she starts forward afresh. Now they are nearly beside Katrinka. Hilda is still in advance, she is almost "home." She has not faltered since that bugle note sent her flying; like an arrow still she is speeding toward the goal. Cheer after cheer rises in the air. Peter is silent, but his eyes shine like stars. "Huzza! Huzza!"

The Crier's voice is heard again.

"Hilda van Gleck—one mile!"

A loud murmur of approval runs through the crowd, catching the music in its course, till all seems one sound, with a glad, rhythmic throbbing in its depths. When the flag waves all is still.

Once more the bugle blows a terrific blast. It sends off the boys like chaff before the wind—dark chaff, I admit, and in big pieces.

It is whisked around at the flag-staff, driven faster yet by the cheers and shouts along the line. We begin, to see what is coming. There are three boys in advance this time, and all abreast. Hans, Peter and Lambert. Carl soon breaks the ranks, rushing through with a whiff! Fly, Hans, fly, Peter, don't let Carl beat again. Carl the bitter, Carl the insolent. Van Mounen is flagging, but you are strong as ever. Hans and Peter, Peter and Hans—which is foremost? We love them both. We scarcely care which is the fleeter.

Hilda, Annie and Gretel, seated upon the long crimson bench, can remain quiet no longer. They spring to their feet— so different, and yet one in eagerness. Hilda instantly reseats herself; none shall know how interested she is, none shall know how anxious, how filled with one hope. Shut your eyes, Hilda— hide your face rippling with joy. Peter has beaten.

"Peter van Holp—one mile!" calls The Crier.

The same buzz of excitement as before, while the judges take notes, the same throbbing of music through the din—

but something is different. A little crowd presses close about some object near the column. Carl has fallen. He is not hurt, though somewhat stunned. If he were less sullen he would find more sympathy in these warm young hearts. As it is they forget him as soon as he is fairly on his feet again.

The girls are to skate their third mile.

How resolute the little maidens look as they stand in a line! Some are solemn with a sense of responsibility, some wear a smile, half bashful, half provoked, but one air of determination pervades them all.

This third mile may decide the race. Still, if neither Gretel nor Hilda win, there is yet a chance among the rest for the silver skates.

Each girl feels sure that this time she will accomplish the distance in one half the time. How they stamp to try their runners, how nervously they examine each strap—how erect they stand at last, every eye upon Madame van Gleck.

The bugle thrills through them again. With quivering eagerness they spring forward, bending, but in perfect balance. Each flashing stroke seems longer than the last.

Now they are skimming off in the distance.

Again the eager straining of eyes—again the shouts and cheering, again the thrill of excitement as, after a few moments, four or five, in advance of the rest, come speeding back, nearer, nearer to the white columns.

Who is first? Not Rychie, Katrinka, Annie, nor Hilda, nor the girl in yellow—but Gretel—Gretel, the fleetest sprite of a girl that ever skated. She was but playing in the earlier race, *now* she is in earnest, or rather something within her has determined to win. That lithe little form makes no effort, but it cannot stop—not until the goal is passed.

In vain The Crier lifts his voice—he cannot be heard. He has no news to tell—it is already ringing through the crowd. *Gretel has won the silver skates!*

Like a bird she has flown over the ice, like a bird she looks about her in a timid, startled way. She longs to dart to the sheltered nook where her father and mother stand. But Hans is beside her—the girls are crowding around. Hilda's kind, joyous voice breathes in her ear. From that hour, none will despise her. Goose-girl or not, Gretel stands acknowledged Queen of the Skaters!

With natural pride Hans turns to see if Peter van Holp is witnessing his sister's triumph. Peter is not looking toward them at all. He is kneeling, bending his troubled face low, and working hastily at his skate-strap. Hans is beside him at once.

"Are you in trouble, mynheer?"

"Ah, Hans! that you? Yes, my fun is over. I tried to tighten my strap—to make a new hole—and this botheration of a knife has cut it nearly in two."

"Mynheer," said Hans, at the same time pulling off a skate—"you must use my strap!"

"Not I, indeed, Hans Brinker," cried Peter, looking up, "though I thank you warmly. Go to your post, my friend, the bugle will sound in a minute."

"Mynheer," pleaded Hans in a husky voice. "You have called me your friend. Take this strap—quick! There is not an instant to lose. I shall not skate this time—indeed, I am out of practice. Mynheer, you *must* take it"—and Hans, blind and deaf to any remonstrance, slipped his strap into Peter's skate and implored him to put it on.

"Come, Peter!" cried Lambert from the line, "we are waiting for you."

"For madame's sake," pleaded Hans, "be quick. She is motioning to you to join the racers. There, the skate is almost on; quick, mynheer, fasten it. I could not possibly win. The race lies between Master Schummel and yourself."

"You are a noble fellow, Hans!" cried Peter, yielding at last. He sprang to his post just as the white handkerchief fell to the ground. The bugle sends forth its blast—loud, clear and ringing.

Off go the boys!

"Mine gott," cries a tough old fellow from Delft. "They beat everything, these Amsterdam youngsters. See them!"

See them indeed! They are winged Mercuries everyone of them. What mad errand are they on? Ah, I know; they are hunting Peter van Holp. He is some fleet-footed runaway from Olympus. Mercury and his troop of winged cousins are in full chase. They will catch him! Now Carl is the runaway—pursuit grows furious—Ben is foremost!

The chase turns into a cloud of mist. It is coming this way. Who is hunted now? Mercury himself. It is Peter, Peter van Holp. Fly, Peter!—Hans is watching you. He is sending all his fleetness, all his strength into your feet. Your mother and sister are pale with eagerness. Hilda is trembling and dare not look up. Fly, Peter!! the crowd has not gone deranged, it is only cheering. The pursuers are close upon you! Touch the white column! It beckons—it is reeling before you—it——

Huzza! Huzza! Peter has won the silver skates!

"Peter van Holp!" shouted The Crier. But who heard him? "Peter van Holp!" shouted a hundred voices, for he was the favorite boy of the place. Huzza! Huzza!

Now the music was resolved to be heard. It struck up

GRETEL GRATEFULLY TOOK THE SKATES AND
FLOWERS IN HER APRON

a lively air, then a tremendous march. The spectators, thinking something new was about to happen, deigned to listen and to look.

The racers formed in single file. Peter, being tallest, stood first. Gretel, the smallest of all, took her place at the end. Hans, who had borrowed a strap from the cake-boy, was near the head.

Three gaily twined arches were placed at intervals upon the river facing the Van Gleck pavilion.

Skating slowly and in perfect time to the music, the boys and girls moved forward, led on by Peter. It was beautiful to see the bright procession glide along like a living creature. It curved and doubled, and drew its graceful length in and out among the arches—whichever way Peter the head went, the body was sure to follow. Sometimes it steered direct for the center arch, then, as if seized with a new impulse, turned away and curled itself about the first one; then unwound slowly and, bending low, with quick, snake-like curvings, crossed the river, passing at length through the furthest arch.

When the music was slow, the procession seemed to crawl like a thing afraid; it grew livelier and the creature darted forward with a spring, gliding rapidly among the arches, in and out, curling, twisting, turning, never losing form until, at the shrill call of the bugle rising above the music, it suddenly resolved itself into boys and girls standing in double semi-circle before Madame van Gleck's pavilion.

Peter and Gretel stand in the center in advance of the others. Madame van Gleck rises majestically. Gretel trembles, but feels that she must look at the beautiful lady. She cannot hear what is said, there is such a buzzing all around her. She is thinking that she ought to try and make a courtesy, such as her mother makes to the meester, when suddenly something so dazzling is placed in her hand that she gives a cry of joy.

Then she ventures to look about her. Peter, too, has something in his hands—"Oh! oh! how splendid!" she cries, and "Oh! how splendid!" is echoed as far as people can see.

Meantime the silver skates flash in the sunshine, throwing dashes of light upon those two happy faces.

Mevrouw van Gend sends a little messenger with her bouquets. One for Hilda, one for Carl, and others for Peter and Gretel.

At sight of the flowers the Queen of the Skaters beomes uncontrollable. With a bright stare of gratitude she gathers skates and bouquet in her apron—hugs them to her bosom, and darts off to search for her father and mother in the scattering crowd.

XXXVII

JOY IN THE COTTAGE

PERHAPS you were surprised to learn that Raff and his vrouw were at the skating race; you would have been more so had you been with them on the evening of that merry twentieth of December. To see the Brinker cottage standing sulkily alone on the frozen marsh, with its bulgy, rheumatic-looking walls, and its slouched hat of a roof pulled far over its eyes, one would never suspect that a lively scene was passing within.

A stray gleam of sunshine slipping down from the willow stump, crept stealthily under the cottage. It seemed to feel that the inmates would give it welcome if it could only get near them. The room under which it hid was as clean as clean could be. The very cracks in the rafters were polished. Delicious odors filled the air. A huge peat fire upon the hearth sent flashes of harmless lightning at the sombre walls. It played in turn upon the great leathern Bible, upon Gretel's closet-bed, the household things on their pegs, and the beautiful silver skates and the flowers upon the table. Dame Brinker's honest face shone and twinkled in the changing light. Gretel and Hans, with arms entwined, were leaning against the fire-place, laughing merrily, and Raff Brinker was dancing!

I do not mean that he was pirouetting or cutting a pigeon-wing, either of which would have been entirely too undignified for the father of a family; I simply affirm that while they were chatting pleasantly together Raff suddenly sprang from his seat, snapped his fingers and performed two or three flourishes very much like the climax of a Highland fling. Next he caught his vrouw in his arms and fairly lifted her from the ground in his delight.

"Huzza!" he cried, "I have it. I have it. It's *Thomas Higgs*. That's the name. It came upon me like a flash; write it down, lad, write it down!"

Someone knocked at the door.

"It's the meester," cried the delighted dame. "Goede Gunst! how things come to pass!"

Mother and children came in merry collision as they rushed to open the door.

It was not the doctor, after all, but three boys—Peter van Holp, Lambert and Ben.

"Good-evening, young gentlemen," said Dame Brinker, so happy and proud that she would scarce have been surprised at a visit from the King himself.

"Good-evening, jufvrouw," said the trio, making magnificent bows.

"Dear me!" thought Dame Brinker, as she bobbed up and down like a churn-dasher, "it's lucky I learned to courtesy at Heidelberg!"

Raff was content to return the boys' salutations with a respectful nod.

"Pray be seated, young masters," said the dame, as Gretel bashfully thrust a stool toward them. "There's lack of chairs, as you see, but this one by the fire is at your service, and if you don't mind the hardness, that oak chest is as good a seat as the best. That's right, Hans, pull it out."

By the time the boys were seated to the dame's satisfaction, Peter, acting as spokesman, had explained that they were going to attend a lecture at Amsterdam and had stopped on the way to return Hans' strap.

"Oh, mynheer," cried Hans earnestly, "it is too much trouble. I am very sorry."

"No trouble at all, Hans; I could have waited for you to come to your work tomorrow had I not wished to call. And, Hans, talking of your work, my father is much pleased with it; a carver by trade could not have done it better. He would like to have the south arbor ornamented also, but I told him you were going to school again."

"Aye!" put in Raff Brinker, emphatically, "Hans must go to school at once—and Gretel as well—that is true."

"I am glad to hear you say so," responded Peter, turning toward the father, "and very glad to know that you are again a well man."

"Yes, young master, a well man and able to work as steady as ever—thank God!"

[Here Hans hastily wrote something on the edge of a time-worn almanac that hung by the chimney-place.] "Aye, that's right, lad; set it down. Figgs! Wiggs! Alack! Alack!" added Raff in great dismay, "it's gone again."

"All right, father," said Hans, "the name's down now in black and white. Here, look at it, father; mayhap the rest will come to you. If we had the place as well it would be complete." Then, turning to Peter, he said in a low tone, "I have an important errand in town, mynheer, and if——"

"Wist!" exclaimed the dame, lifting her hands, "not to Amsterdam tonight, and you've owned your legs were aching under you. Nay, nay—it'll be soon enough to go at early daylight."

"Daylight indeed!" echoed Raff, "that would never do. Nay, Meitje, he must go this hour."

Just then Peter drew a long strap from his pocket.

Handing it to Hans he said in an undertone, "I need not thank you for lending me this, Hans Brinker. Such boys as you do not ask for thanks—but I must say you did me a great kindness, and I am proud to acknowledge it. I did not know," he added laughingly, "until fairly in the race, how anxious I was to win."

Hans was glad to join in Peter's laugh—it covered his embarrassment and gave his face a chance to cool off a little. Honest, generous boys like Hans have such a stupid way of blushing when you least expect it.

"It was nothing, mynheer," said the dame, hastening to her son's relief, "the lad's whole soul was in having you win the race, I know it was!"

This helped matters beautifully.

"Ah, mynheer," Hans hurried to say, "from the first start I felt stiff and strange on my feet; I was well out of it so long as I had no chance of winning."

Peter looked rather distressed.

"We may hold different opinions there. That part of the business troubles me. It is too late to mend it now, but it would be really a kindness to me if——"

The rest of Peter's speech was uttered so confidentially that I cannot record it. Enough to say, Hans soon started back in dismay, and Peter, looking very much ashamed, stammered out something to the effect that he would keep them, since he won the race, but it was "all wrong."

Here Van Mounen coughed, as if to remind Peter that lecture-hour was approaching fast. At the same moment Ben laid something upon the table.

"Ah," exclaimed Peter, "I forgot my other errand. Your sister ran off so quickly today that Madame van Gleck had no opportunity to give her the case for her skates."

"S-st!" said Dame Brinker, shaking her head reproachfully at Gretel, "she was a very rude girl, I'm sure." [Secretly she was thinking that very few women had such a fine little daughter.]

"No, indeed," laughed Peter, "she did exactly the right thing—ran home with her richly won treasures—who would not? Don't let us detain you, Hans," he continued, turning around as he spoke; but Hans, who was eagerly watching the father, seemed to have forgotten their presence.

Meantime Raff, lost in thought, was repeating under his breath, "Thomas Higgs—Thomas Higgs; aye, that's the name. Alack! if I could but tell the place as well."

The skate-case was elegantly made of crimson morocco, ornamented with silver. If a fairy had breathed upon its tiny key, or Jack Frost himself designed its delicate tracery, they could not have been more daintily beautiful. *"For the Fleetest"* was written upon the cover in sparkling letters. It was lined with velvet and in one corner was stamped the name and address of the maker.

Gretel thanked Peter in her own simple way; then, being quite delighted and confused, and not knowing what else to do, lifted the case, carefully examining it in every part. "It's made by Mynheer Birmingham," she said after awhile, still blushing and holding it before her eyes.

"Birmingham!" replied Lambert van Mounen, "that's the name of a place in England. Let me see it."

"Ha! ha!" he laughed, holding the open case toward the firelight, "no wonder you thought so, but it's a slight mistake.

The case was made at Birmingham, but the maker's name is in smaller letters.   Humph! they're so small I can't read them!"

"Let me try," said Peter, leaning over his shoulder. "Why, man, it's perfectly distinct.   It's T—H—it's T——"

"Well!" exclaimed Lambert triumphantly, "if you can read it so easily, let's hear it; T—H what?"

"T. H.—T. H.   Oh! why, Thomas Higgs, to be sure," replied Peter, pleased to be able to decipher it at last.   Then, feeling they had been behaving rather unceremoniously, he turnd toward Hans—

Peter turned pale!   What was the matter with the people? Raff and Hans had started up and were staring at him in glad amazement.   Gretel looked wild.   Dame Brinker, with an unlighted candle in her hand, was rushing about the room, crying, "Hans! Hans! where's your hat? Oh, the meester! Oh, the meester!"

"Birmingham! Higgs!" exclaimed Hans.   "Did you say Higgs? we've found him! I must be off."

"You see, young masters," panted the dame, at the same time snatching Hans' hat from the bed, "you see—we know him—he's our—no, he isn't—I mean—oh, Hans, you must go to Amsterdam this minute!"

"Good-night, mynheers," panted Hans, radiant with sudden joy, "good-night—you will excuse me, I must go. Birmingham—Higgs—Higgs—Birmingham," and, seizing his hat from his mother and his skates from Gretel, he rushed from the cottage.

What could the boys think but that the entire Brinker family had suddenly gone crazy!

They bade an embarrassed "Good-evening" and turned to go. But Raff stopped them.

"This Thomas Higgs, young masters, is a—a person."

"Ah!" exclaimed Peter, quite sure that Raff was the most crazy of all.

"Yes—a person—a—ahem!—a friend. We thought him dead. I hope it is the same man. In England, did you say?"

"Yes, Birmingham," answered Peter, "it must be Birmingham in England."

"I know the man," said Ben, addressing Lambert. "His factory is not four miles from our place—a queer fellow—still as an oyster—don't seem at all like an Englishman. I've often seen him—a solemn-looking chap, with magnificent eyes. He made a beautiful writing-case once for me to give Jenny on her birthday—makes pocketbooks, telescope cases, and all kinds of leather work."

As this was said in English, Van Mounen of course translated it for the benefit of all concerned, noticing meanwhile that neither Raff nor his vrouw looked very miserable, though Raff was trembling and the dame's eyes were swimming with tears.

You may believe the doctor heard every word of the story when later in the evening he came driving back with Hans. "The three young gentlemen had gone some time," Dame Brinker said, "but like enough, by hurrying, it would be easy to find them coming out from the lecture, wherever that was."

"True," said Raff, nodding his head, "the vrouw always hits upon the right thing. It would be well to see the young English gentleman, mynheer, before he forgets all about Thomas Higgs—it's a slippery name, d'ye see?—one can't hold it safe a minute. It came upon me sudden and strong as a pile-driver, and my boy writ it down. Aye, mynheer, I'd haste to talk with the English lad; he's seen your son many a time—only to think on't!"

Dame Brinker took up the thread of the discourse.

"You'll pick out the lad quick enough, mynheer, because he's in company with Master Peter van Holp; and his hair curls all up over his forehead like foreign folks', and, if you hear him speak, he talks kind of big and fast, only it's English, but that wouldn't be any hindrance to your honor."

The doctor had already lifted his hat to go.   With a beaming face he muttered something about it's being just like the young scamp to give himself a rascally English name; called Hans "my son"—thereby making that young gentleman happy as a lord—and left the cottage with very little ceremony, considering what a great meester he was.

The grumbling coachman comforted himself by speaking his mind, as he drove back to Amsterdam.   Since the doctor was safely stowed away in the coach and could not hear a word, it was a fine time to say terrible things of folks who hadn't no manner of feeling for nobody, and who were always wanting the horses a dozen times of a night.

XXXVIII

THE MYSTERY OF THOMAS HIGGS

HIGGS' factory was a mine of delight for the gossips of Birmingham. It was a small building, but quite large enough to hold a mystery. Who the proprietor was, or where he came from, none could tell. He looked like a gentleman—that was certain—though everybody knew he had risen from an apprenticeship; and he could handle his pen like a writing-master.

Years ago he had suddenly appeared in the place a lad of eighteen—learned his trade faithfully, and risen in the confidence of his employer—been taken in as a partner soon after his time was up—and finally, when old Willet died, had assumed the business on his own hands. This was all that was known of his affairs.

His nationality was a great puzzle. The English name spoke plainly enough for *one* side of his house, but of what manner of nation was his mother? If she'd been an American he'd certainly have high cheekbones and reddish skin; if a German, he would have known the language, and Squire Smith declared he didn't; if French it would come out in his speech. There was nothing he could be but Dutch. And, strangest of all, though the man always pricked up his ears when you talked of Holland, he didn't seem to know the first thing about the country when you put him to the point.

Anyhow, as no letters ever came to him from his mother's family in Holland, and as nobody living had ever seen old Higgs, the family couldn't be anything much. Probably Thomas Higgs himself was no better than he should be, for all he pretended to carry himself so straight; and for their parts, the gossips declared, they were not going to trouble their heads about him. Consequently Thomas Higgs and his affairs were never-failing subjects of discussion.

Picture, then, the consternation among all the good people when it was announced by "somebody who was there and ought to know," that the post-boy had that very morning handed Higgs a foreign-looking letter and the man had "turned as white as the wall, rushed to his factory, talked a bit with one of the head workmen and, without bidding a creature good-bye, was off, bag and baggage, before you could wink, ma'am." Mistress Scrubbs, his landlady, was in deep affliction.

Whereupon her dearest friend, Miss Scrumpkins, ran home to tell all about it. And, as everybody knew the Scrumpkinses, a shining gossamer of news was soon woven from one end of the street to the other.

An investigating committee met, that evening, at Mrs. Snigham's—sitting, in secret session, over her best china. Though invited only to a quiet "tea," the amount of judicial business they transacted on the occasion was prodigious. The biscuits were actually cold before the committee had a chance to eat anything. There was so much to talk over—and it was so important that it should be firmly established that each member had always been "certain sure that something extraordinary would be happening to that man yet," that it was near eight o'clock before Mrs. Snigham gave anybody a second cup.

XXXIX

BROAD SUNSHINE

ONE snowy day in January, Laurens Boekman went with his father to pay his respects to the Brinker family.

Raff was resting after the labors of the day; Gretel having filled and lighted his pipe, was brushing every speck of ash from the hearth; the dame was spinning; and Hans, perched upon a stool by the window, was diligently studying his lessons—a peaceful, happy household whose main excitement during the past week had been the looking forward to this possible visit from Thomas Higgs.

As soon as the grand presentation was over, Dame Brinker insisted upon giving her guests some hot tea; it was enough to freeze anyone, she said, to be out in such crazy, blustering weather. While they were talking with her husband she whispered to Gretel that the young gentleman's eyes and her boy's were certainly as much alike as four beans, to say nothing of a way they both had of looking as if they were stupid and yet knew as much as a body's grandfather.

Gretel was disappointed. She had looked forward to a tragic scene, such as Annie Bouman had often described to her, from story-books; and here was the gentleman who came so near being a murderer, who for ten years had been wandering over the face of the earth, who had believed himself deserted and scorned by his father—the very young gentleman who had fled from his country in such magnificent trouble, sitting by the fire just as pleasant and natural as could be!

To be sure his voice had trembled when he talked with her parents and he had met his father's look with a bright kind of smile that would have suited a dragonkiller bringing the waters of perpetual youth to his king—but after all he wasn't at all like the conquering hero in Annie's book.

All things considered, Gretel was disappointed. Raff, however, was perfectly satisfied. The message was delivered; Doctor Boekman had his son safe and sound, and the poor lad had done nothing sinful after all, except in thinking his father would have abandoned him for an accident. To be sure, the graceful stripling had become rather a heavy man—Raff had unconsciously hoped to clasp that same boyish hand again—but all things were changed to Raff, for that matter. So he pushed back every feeling but joy, as he saw father and son sitting side by side at his hearthstone. Meantime, Hans was wholly occupied in the thought of Thomas Higgs' happiness in being able to be the meester's assistant again; and Dame Brinker was sighing softly to herself wishing that the lad's mother were alive to see him—such a fine young gentleman as he was, and wondering how Doctor Boekman could bear to see the silver watch getting so dull. He had worn it ever since Raff had handed it over, that was evident. What had he done with the gold one he used to wear?

The light was shinning full upon Doctor Boekman's face. How contented he looked; how much younger and brighter than formerly. The hard lines were quite melting away. He was laughing, as he said to the father:

"Am I not a happy man, Raff Brinker? My son will sell out his factory this month and open a warehouse in Amsterdam. I shall have all my spectacle cases for nothing."

Hans started from his reverie. "A warehouse, mynheer! and will Thomas Higgs—I mean—is your son not to be your assistant again?"

A shade passed over the meester's face, but he brightened with an effort as he replied:

"Oh, no, Laurens has had quite enough of that. He wishes to be a merchant."

Hans appeared so surprised and disappointed that his friend asked good-naturedly:

"Why so silent, boy? Is it any disgrace to be a merchant?"

"N—not a disgrace, mynheer," stammered Hans, "but——"

"But what?"

"Why, the other calling is so much better," answered Hans, "so much nobler. I think, mynheer," he added, kindling with enthusiasm, "that to be a surgeon, to cure the sick and crippled, to save human life, to be able to do what you have done for my father—is the grandest thing on earth."

The doctor was regarding him sternly. Hans felt rebuked. His cheeks were flushed; hot tears were gathering under his lashes.

"It is an ugly business, boy, this surgery," said the doctor, still frowning at Hans, "it requires great patience, self-denial and perseverance."

"I am sure it does," cried Hans, kindling again. "It calls for wisdom, too, and a reverence for God's work. Ah, mynheer, it may have its trials and drawbacks—but you do not mean what you say—it is great and noble, not ugly! Pardon me, mynheer. It is not for me to speak so boldly."

Doctor Boekman was evidently displeased. He · turned his back on the boy and conferred aside with Laurens. Meanwhile the dame scowled a terrible warning at Hans. These great people, she knew well enough, never like to hear poor folk speak up so pert.

The meester turned around.

"How old are you, Hans Brinker?"

"Fifteen, mynheer," was the startled reply.

"Would you like to become a physician?"

"Yes, mynheer," answered Hans, quivering with excitement.

"Would you be willing, with your parents' consent, to devote yourself to study, to go to the University—and, in time, to be a student in my office?"

"*Yes,* mynheer."

"You would not grow restless, think you, and change your mind just as I had set my heart upon preparing you to be my successor?"

Hans' eyes flashed.

"You may believe him there," cried the dame, who could remain quiet no longer, "Hans is like a rock when once he decides; and as for study, mynheer, the child has almost grown fast to his books of late. He can jumble off Latin already, like any priest."

The doctor smiled. "Well, Hans, I see nothing to prevent us from carrying out this plan, if your father agrees."

"Ahem," said Raff, too proud of his boy to be very meek. "The fact is, mynheer, I prefer an active, out-of-door life myself. But if the lad's inclined to study for a meester and he'd have the benefit of your good word to push him on in the world, it's all one to me. The money's all that's a-wanting, but it mightn't be long, with two strong pair of arms to earn it, before we——"

"Tut! tut!" interrupted the doctor, "if I take your right-hand man away I must pay the cost, and glad enough will I be to do it. It will be like having *two* sons—eh, Laurens? One a merchant and the other a surgeon—I shall be the happiest man in Holland! Come to me in the morning, Hans, and we will arrange matters at once."

Hans bowed assent. He dared not trust himself to speak.

"And, Brinker," continued the doctor, "my son Laurens will need a trusty, ready man like you when he opens his warehouse in Amsterdam; someone to overlook matters and see that the lazy clowns round about the place do their duty. Someone to—— Why don't you tell him yourself, you rascal!!"

This last was addressed to the son and did not sound half as fierce as it looks in print. The rascal and Raff soon understood each other perfectly.

"I'm loath to leave the dykes," said the latter, after they had talked together awhile, "but you have made me such a good offer, mynheer, I'd be robbing my family if I let it go past me."

———

Take a long look at Hans as he sits there staring gratefully at the meester, for you shall not see him again for many years.

And Gretel—ah, what a vista of puzzling work suddenly opens before her! Yes, for dear Hans' sake she will study now. If he really is to be a meester, his sister must not shame his greatness.

How faithfully those glancing eyes shall yet seek for the jewels that lie hidden in rocky school-books! And how they shall yet brighten and droop at the coming of one whom she knows of now, only as the boy who wore a red cap on that wonderful day when she found the silver skates in her apron!

But the doctor and Laurens are going. Dame Brinker is making her best courtesy. Raff stands beside her, looking every inch a man as he grasps the meester's hand. Through the open cottage door we can look out upon the level Dutch landscape all alive with the falling snow.

CONCLUSION

OUR story is nearly told. Time passes in Holland just as surely and steadily as here; in that respect no country is odd. To the Brinker family it has brought great changes; Hans has spent the years faithfully and profitably, conquering obstacles as they arose, and pursuing one object with all the energy of his nature. If often the way has been rugged, his resolution has never failed. Sometimes he echoes, with his good old friend, the words said long ago in that little cottage near Broek: "Surgery is an ugly business," but always in his heart of hearts lingers the echo of those truer words, "It is great and noble! it awakes a reverence for God's work!"

Were you in Amsterdam today you might see the famous Doctor Brinker riding in his grand coach to visit his parents; or, it might be, you would see him skating with his own boys and girls upon the frozen canal. For Annie Bouman, the beautiful, frank-hearted peasant girl, you would inquire in vain; but Annie Brinker, the vrouw of the great physician, is very like her—only, as Hans says, she is even lovelier, wiser, more like a fairy godmother than ever.

Peter van Holp also is a married man. I could have told you before that he and Hilda would join hands and glide through life together, just as years ago they skimmed side by side over the frozen, sunlit river.

At one time I came near hinting that Katrinka and Carl would join hands. It is fortunate now that the report was not started, for Katrinka changed her mind and is single to this day. The lady is not quite so merry as formerly and, I grieve to say, some of the tinkling bells are out of tune. But she is the life of her social circle still. I wish she would be in earnest, just for a little while; but no, it is not her nature. Her cares and sorrows do nothing more than disturb the tinkling; they never waken any deeper music.

Rychie's soul has been stirred to its depths during these long years. Her history would tell how seed carelessly sown is sometimes reaped in anguish, and how a golden harvest may follow a painful planting. If I mistake not, you may be able to read the written record before long; that is, if you are familiar with the Dutch language. In the witty but earnest author whose words are welcomed at this day in thousands of Holland homes, few could recognize the haughty, flippant Rychie who scoffed at little Gretel.

Lambert van Mounen and Ludwig van Holp are good Christian men and, what is more easily to be seen at a glance, thriving citizens. Both are dwellers in Amsterdam, but one clings to the old city of that name and the other is a pilgrim to the new. Van Mounen's present home is not far from

Central Park and he says if the New Yorkers do their duty the park will, in time, equal his beautiful Bosch, near The Hague. He often thinks of the Katrinka of his boyhood, but he is glad now that Katrinka, the woman, sent him away; though it seemed at the time his darkest hour. Ben's sister Jennie has made him very happy, happier than he could have been with anyone else in the wide world.

Carl Schummel has had a hard life. His father met with reverses in business, and as Carl had not many warm friends, and above all was not sustained by noble principles, he has been tossed about by Fortune's battledore until his gayest feathers are nearly all knocked off. He is a bookkeeper in the thriving Amsterdam house of Boekman and Schimmelpenninck. Voostenwalbert, the junior partner, treats him kindly, and he in turn is very respectful to the "monkey with a long name for a tail."

Of all our group of Holland friends, Jacob Poot is the only one who has passed away. Good-natured, true-hearted and unselfish to the last, he is mourned now as heartily as he was loved and laughed at while on earth. He grew to be very thin before he died; thinner than Benjamin Dobbs, who is now portliest among the portly.

Raff Brinker and his vrouw have been living comfortably in Amsterdam for many years—a faithful happy pair, as simple and straightforward in their good fortune as they were patient and trustful in darker days. They have a summer-house near the old cottage and thither they often repair with their children and grandchildren on the pleasant summer afternoons when the pond-lilies rear their queenly heads above the water.

The story of Hans Brinker would be but half told if we did not leave him with Gretel standing near. Dear, quick, patient little Gretel! What is she now? Ask old Doctor Boekman: he will declare she is the finest singer, the loveliest woman in Amsterdam. Ask Hans and Annie, they will assure you she is the dearest sister ever known. Ask her husband— he who wore the red cap on the day of the grand skating race: he will tell you she is the brightest, sweetest little wife in Holland. Ask Dame Brinker and Raff: their eyes will glisten with joyous tears. Ask the poor: the air will be filled with blessings.

But, lest you forget a tiny form trembling and sobbing on the mound before the Brinker cottage, ask the Van Glecks; they will never weary telling of the darling little girl who won The Silver Skates.

COSIMO CLASSICS

COSIMO is an innovative publisher of books and publications that inspire, inform and engage readers worldwide. Our titles are drawn from a range of subjects including health, business, philosophy, history, science and sacred texts. We specialize in using print-on-demand technology (POD), making it possible to publish books for both general and specialized audiences and to keep books in print indefinitely. With POD technology new titles can reach their audiences faster and more efficiently than with traditional publishing.

> ➢ **Permanent Availability:** Our books & publications never go out-of-print.

> ➢ **Global Availability:** Our books are always available online at popular retailers and can be ordered from your favorite local bookstore.

COSIMO CLASSICS brings to life unique, rare, out-of-print classics representing subjects as diverse as *Alternative Health, Business and Economics, Eastern Philosophy, Personal Growth, Mythology, Philosophy, Sacred Texts, Science, Spirituality* and much more!

COSIMO-on-DEMAND publishes your books, publications and reports. If you are an Author, part of an Organization, or a Benefactor with a publishing project and would like to bring books back into print, publish new books fast and effectively, would like your publications, books, training guides, and conference reports to be made available to your members and wider audiences around the world, we can assist you with your publishing needs.

Visit our website at www.cosimobooks.com to learn more about Cosimo, browse our catalog, take part in surveys or campaigns, and sign-up for our newsletter.

And if you wish please drop us a line at info@cosimobooks.com. We look forward to hearing from you.